CULLIGAN'S WALK

CULLIGAN'S WALK

Being the chronical of William Culligan's journey from the
1840's into the 1880's, written in the prevalent style of that
historical period.

John Woods

Woods publishing   Tucson, Arizona

This edition was prepared for publication by
Ghost River Images
5350 East Fourth Street
Tucson, Arizona 85711
www.ghostriverimages.com

Cover background photograph
courtesy of U.S.B.L.M.

ISBN 978-1-7338435-0-8

Library of Congress Control Number: 2019903229

Printed in the United States of America
March 2019

Contents

Dedication

For Bunker de France

Thanks Bunker. Couldn't have done it without you.

Chapter One

On a hot day, after the close of the Civil War, the orphaned girl stood high on the bank looking out to sea, she saw a lifeboat under sail and headed for this beach.

The lifeboat held three men—unmoving—like rocks. The fourth man was a boulder.

Larco was manning the tiller when they crunched up on shore. Culligan had outweighed each of the men in the boat by at least forty pounds and being on the same water-ration as the smaller men had been almost fatal. He could do no more than sit where he was, nauseous and faint, with bowed head and wondering, *where are we?*

Two others had died of exposure while the two would-be mutineers had been killed.

• • •

Barefoot, the girl ran down the bank and into the lapping waves while Rendel and Isler poured themselves out of the bow and onto dry land.

Culligan, astern, sat anchored to his seat. He heard a girl's voice, sounding far off, saying, "You dead Suh?" He looked up and saw a skinny young black child waist high in the water and close enough to touch. He looked directly into her eyes, and realizing she was real, he would have smiled if he could. He croaked, "Not yet girl. Not yet!"

Seaman Larco, a smallish man and older than Culligan, went over the side. Without speaking, Larco and the girl helped Culligan, his being too dehydrated and hurting to move well, over the side and up onto the beach and They stretched him out on the only piece of shade there was.

The girl fetched him fresh water.

When Culligan awoke, the girl was sitting to the left of his head and bathing his face with a wet rag. His head then turned towards her and she gave him another drink of water. He saw where his Remington revolver was sitting on a piece of dry driftwood. How it got there he did not remember.

In the loneliness of his time in deep woods, Culligan had dreamed of rescuing a fair-haired and blue-eyed young maid. He realized, *now I'm the one being rescued . . . and by a scrawny young black girl.*

The girl provided the men with fresh water. Larco said to her, "Can you get us help?" She nodded, then began the climb up the sandy bank.

• • •

When Cassy (that was the child's name) came running up to his wagon, Buddy Felton raised the buggy whip to warn her off. She halted, but only for a moment before again running after the wagon. He halted the mule and barked, "I have nothing to give you!" He raised the whip again. She ducked away and pointing she screamed, "White men!" Now that, Buddy understood.

When Cassy was excited she spoke Gulla, a language most whites did not understand, but Buddy was able to figure it out.

• • •

Buddy arrived above the bank with mule and wagon. The men below had managed a small measure of recovery, and with Larco and Cassy's help, Culligan rose to his feet. When Larco handed Culligan his handgun, he lifted his shirt, and seated the short-barreled Remington in his belly holster.

Rendel, Isler, Larco, and Culligan staggered up to the top of the bank. Buddy Felton said, "Only the dead look as sorry as you men. Where did you all come from?" Larco said, "About halfway between here and Africa. We been in a lifeboat for 36 days. What is this place?"

"South Carolina. The town of Belting is down the road a piece."

Away from the beach the air was hot and still. While Felton and Cassy had sweat running down their faces, the men from the lifeboat had nothing left to sweat. Larco said, "We could use some help."

"You sure do look it. Get up in the wagon. I can get you to Belting."

Once the men climbed into the wagon, Culligan saw Cassy standing and not knowing what to do. He reached out his hand and mumbled, "Girl, take my hand and get yourself up in this here wagon."

Buddy looked at Culligan.

He looked back. "I intend to pay you and this girl for your kindness."

Buddy nodded, as if he believed it would ever happen. "When the war ended I was twenty-six year res old and laying up in the hospital after losing my leg. Any of you fellows in the war?"

"Three of us," Larco said, "was on the other side of the world, while the big fella was prospecting up in Canada till war's end."

Buddy Felton nodded. "The Union Army marched through our farm and took every one of our pigs, our milk cow, all our chickens—we can grow food but no money crop."

Larco said, "They didn't get your mule?"

"My brother Johnny was eleven and hid the mule back in deep woods."

Larco nodded, "Good for him."

"So now," Buddy said, "I scare up some small sums hauling freight."

The road to Belting aimed itself North and directly at a huge and ancient oak tree, then reared itself eastward and halfway around the tree before heading off again in a northern direction. West of that huge tree, it being called Grandfather Oak, stood the Baptist Church. Two dogs barked their welcome. The second building was a bare and weather- beaten hotel and Rendel and Isler rolled out of the wagon and entered.

Rendel and Isler separating themselves from Culligan and Larco

. . . and neither minded. Aboard ship, and in the lifeboat, those two had not carried their own weight.

The next building was a saloon, the fourth was a livery stable, then there was a burned-out empty space where a storehouse for farm produce had once stood. Past that burned-out space stood the general store. Not one building in that town had a lick of paint.

At some point, while in that lifeboat, or maybe even before the lifeboat, without saying much, Larco and Culligan had partnered up. Larco looked to Culligan and said, "Now what?"

Culligan pointed.

Buddy Felton delivered Larco, Cassy, and Culligan to the store.

Culligan, coming off the wagon, staggered while fishing a twenty dollar gold piece out of his pocket, Larco steadied him while he turned it over to Buddy, who stared at the coin in his hand. This was more money than he had seen in six years. Recovering himself, Buddy wished them well and then made haste to gather up his younger brother. Buddy and his young brother then returned to the lifeboat and laid claim to it.

• • •

The storekeeper, known as Uncle Josh, winced when two bedraggled white men, followed by a young black girl, staggered into his store. The store had a scale for weighing produce, a grinder for making coffee grounds and cornmeal, there were bins, now almost empty, for holding rice, corn, and beans. Uncle Josh said, "As you can see, my shelves are almost bare. You two are in bad a shape but damn, I can't give you any credit."

Culligan fumbled a twenty dollar gold piece out on the counter and pointed to the single loaf of bread.

Surprised, Uncle Josh handed over the bread. Culligan pushed it over to Larco and said, "Cut to thirds." Larco broke out his Barlow knife, cut the loaf into thirds, pointed to the girl, and Culligan nodded yes.

Culligan croaked, "This girl has done us much kindness. We need shelter for the three of us along with food and blankets. I'll be paying for everything, and make no mistake, I may be weakened, but I shoot straight and this girl has my protection."

Uncle Josh nodded. "Take the storeroom out back. It's been empty two years now. You fellows sure do look terrible."

Larco nodded, "Feel terrible. We need a bucket of water, a tin dipper, food, and bedding," Uncle Josh said, "The water I can get you now. The other things shortly." The storeroom was small, dusty, hot, and had no window. Uncle Josh provided water, three straw ticks to sleep on, and three blankets. There was barely room to lay out the three ticks. Cassy would be sleeping in a room with two white men. She gave no sign, but her fear was real.

Uncle Josh's sister, the widow Hetty Baldwin, showed up with a pot of chicken and rice soup along with three cups and three spoons. Culligan dipped his cup, motioned to Cassy to dip her cup, and then Larco filled his cup. Stomachs rumbled.

Later, Hetty Baldwin returned for the pot, cups, and spoons. She was a woman about Larco's age, about his size, and Larco thought she was decent enough looking. He followed her outside and said, "Miss Hetty, can you tell us anything about our little black girl?"

"She's probably alone, has no idea who her parents are, and like the others now freed, she's probably living mostly on the eggs of nesting birds, shellfish, and whatever she can steal." Hetty glowered, "Whatever you men want of her she will do."

"That girl brought us water! What we want of her is the chance to repay her kindness!"

"If that is true then I apologize."

"Accepted."

The sun began to set and Cassy was fearful. White folks were feeding her and she knew she would have to pay.

Larco and Culligan, both orphaned at an early age, had recognized in Cassy, another orphan. Still, Larco asked, "Girl, you have family?" She shook her head, thought, *I'm not going to run. I'm too hungry and I'm not going to run.*

"Larco and me," Culligan said, "are likely to sleep heavy. Cassy, you hear anyone moving around out there, anything, you pound on me good and wake me up. You hear?"

• • •

The next day, having eaten and slept stretched out flat, Larco and Culligan's joints still creaked, and their voices were still a rattle, but they were better. Culligan talked to Uncle Josh. "I been thinking on it. Find this girl a decent pair of boots and clothing that will allow her to sit a horse. Get her a coat and hat and whatever else a girl might need and I'll be paying for everything."

Uncle Josh blinked. "You have money, but you sure don't look it." Then he said, "I can do that."

• • •

With the arrival of Rendel, Isler, Larco, and Culligan, four men with money in their pockets, the store's shelves, already low on the necessities, were stripped down to almost nothing.

Four days later, Rendel and Isler headed out. Larco and Culligan were not sorry to see the last of them.

Uncle Josh said, "I have to go to Charleston for supplies. The South is dirt poor and the interest suppliers charge is more than I can charge my customers."

Culligan nodded, said, "How much you owe?"

Uncle Josh thought, *should I tell him?* "Almost two hundred dollars."

Culligan's tired eyebrows managed to rise. "That's a lot! Who will be minding the store?"

"My sister Hetty Baldwin will cook for you and be taking care of the store til I get back. Rendel and Isler told how you killed the mutineers. Those two did not much appreciate you taking up with a colored—said it made them look bad—but won't say more since they're scared of you. You killed the two would-be mutineers?"

"This much," Culligan said, "I will say, the money Rendel and Isler have came out of the pockets of two dead mutineers, while the money in my pocket came up from out of the ground.

"While in Charleston" . . . Culligan handed Uncle Josh four one-hundred dollar bills and Uncle Josh's eyes grew big, "you can pay off the interest you owe. Then find me a Spencer carbine, 56/56 or 56/50, plus 500 rounds of cartridges, the Yellowboy 1866 Winchester with 500 rounds for Larco, and a tent big enough to keep the three of us out of the rain. Also, I need a cartridge belt that will house the 56 caliber round. Get a cartridge belt for Larco that will hold the 44 cartridge and don't forget to pick us up three canteens. I don't ever again want to be without water."

• • •

Culligan and Larco spent time stretched out in the shade provided by Grandfather Oak—while Cassy hovered nearby.

Larco said, "How come you carry a short-barreled Remington instead of the Colt?"

"The Colt has a grip that fits my hand better than the Remington, but not that much better. After I've emptied the Remington, I can drop out my emptied cylinder and drop in a pre-loaded cap'n ball cylinder in about seven seconds. Can't do that with a Colt."

• • •

More than a week had passed. The knots in Culligan's calves were smoothing out, the cramps in his back had loosened, and he was now moving almost as well as the smaller Larco. From time to time, either Culligan or Larco dropped by the store. Culligan said, "Larco, I see you get Hetty Baldwin to laughing, even though she doesn't have much to laugh about, her having lost everything, including a burned-out house and a dead husband. You have that way with you. You even get Cassy to laughing."

"Uh huh. Look at her out there making friends with that puppy. A town this poor, it surprises me that puppy didn't end up in a stewpot. Cully, the way Cassy looks at you—she turns to me for company—but those times when she's frightened, she looks to you."

At dusk, Hetty provided them with a small pitcher of goat's milk. Days later, Culligan said, "Larco, you look like a man would like to stay here and commence courting-up Hetty Baldwin."

Looking off in the distance, Larco said, "Evening time, fireflies are coming out . . . I always did like fireflies."

Culligan nodded. "First time I ever saw fireflies."

"Cully, I can't stay. First off, there's nothing in this town a seaman like me would know how to do, and knowing the feelings they have about me being friends with Cassy, I keep this Derringer close to hand. Hetty is a fine woman and she suits me fine. She tells me she does not understand how we came to be partnered up, you being a big man and me being a small man, me being a likeable sort and you being not so friendly. How did this happen?"

Culligan thought on it. "Jeremiah Doty. He was about as big as you and a decent enough man. I made a gold strike upriver and we sailed together down the Fraser River to Vancouver, BC. That trip got me used to having company."

• • •

"Hetty," Larco said, "seeing how we relate to Cassy, told me that when she was a girl her best friend had been Loren Smith, a black girl her own age. When they got to be a little past Cassy's age, started turning into women, Hetty being white and Loren being black, they couldn't be friends anymore."

Sitting on the porch steps, Culligan looked up at the clouds drifting by. "Good friends are hard to come by. Damn shame when you have to give them up. A long time ago, on a day like this, back on Rosebud Creek in California, Murietta's gang raided our gold camp—the Affleck brothers and I stood together—Murietta rode in first and got past us but me and the Affleck brothers, we killed the next four riding in and that drove off Murietta's gang. In that lifeboat you knew them as the Bishop Brothers. In California they were known as the Affleck Brothers."

"They changed their names?"

"They were wanted for robbery murder in California, but in that lifeboat we were still friends right up to the day they asked me to join with them in taking over. Then we weren't friends anymore." Culligan picked up a small rock and pitched it at the ditch.

"I saw," Larco said. "They went for their guns but you were quicker."

"And I killed two men who had befriended me when I was a boy alone. Damn shame the way things turned out."

Chapter Two—The Preacher comes calling

"Larco," Hetty said, "you going back to sea?"

He shook his head saying, "Hetty, I been to sea all my life and that's pretty much all I know, but that was the third ship to sink out from under me. The second time an explosion blew me off the ship and I had a long swim of nearly two miles, but when I got to shore I didn't give it a second thought and signed up on another ship first chance I had. My luck has been strung out way too thin. I never heard of any seaman, except me, surviving three shipwrecks—much less four.

"Culligan and I seem to have partnered up. We'll be headed out west, taking Cassy with us."

"You'll be taking the black child with you?"

"We will."

"Why?"

"She brought us water."

"What about me?" Hetty said.

"God knows I hunger to settle down with a woman, and Hetty, you are one fine woman. I worked on a chicken farm when I was a boy. I'm not all that fond of chickens, but I liked those chickens a whole lot more than I liked the chicken farmer—I was not much older than Cassy when I ran away to sea and that is all I've done since. Culligan will keep Cassy safe, I'll help, but most of all, I need to find a way to support myself on land, find a way to support you and me before I can ask for your hand."

Hetty nodded. "I have thought on it. You are a decent and handsome enough man Larco, and this land is full of widows. You set yourself up so the living is not too hard for a woman my age and it would pleasure me to be your woman."

• • •

The air was hot and muggy on the day Uncle Josh stepped off the stagecoach. He was not a young man, but even so,on this day his step was light as a feather. Hetty and Uncle Josh got busy unloading supplies and restocking the shelves.

Cassy entered the store with Larco and Culligan. Uncle Josh looked up and presented Cassy with a stick of hard candy. "Culligan, your order is stacked over in the corner. I paid off what I owed, which was 197 dollars, and knowing your plans to travel out West, I picked up two decent saddlebags and a hatchet, along with the tent, cleaning gear, the Spencer, Winchester, cartridges, a tent, plus the three canteens you ordered."

"I appreciate."

Cassy never let Larco and Culligan out of her sight. The three of them walked a mile out of Belting to check out the Carbines.

Larco had never fired a gun and yet, even at his age, still having good eyesight and a steady hand, after he settled down and fired a few more rounds, Culligan saw that Larco, was already about as good a shot with the Winchester as most men could ever be. Most men, in a gunfight, would rattle, take their eyes off their gunsights and onto the man, and might as well be shooting at the moon for all the good it would do. It was clear to Culligan that Larco would not rattle.

• • •

When the three of them went for a walk on the beach, looking out to sea, they saw Buddy and Johnny Felton fighting to manage their sail. Looking to Larco, Culligan said, "You willing to give those fellows a hand–teach them a few things?"

"Uh huh. They sure do need it."

Larco walked down to the water's edge, pointed his Winchester up at the sky, and squeezed off a shot. Johnny and Buddy looked in his direction, he waved to them to come ashore, and then handed the Winchester over to Culligan. With the wind directly behind them, they let the boom out and steered to where Larco was standing on the beach. Larco waded out, climbed aboard and said, "I been under sail all my life . . . You fellows are just getting started . . .."

Cassy did not need to know sailing and Culligan had already lived it, so Culligan and Cassy moved away to laze out on the beach and watch the boat's progress. Culligan was enjoying being able to rest but then rose to go behind the dune and pee. When he came off that lifeboat he was so dehydrated that when he started drinking water and could pee again, it came out brackish. With his every day now drinking lots of water he saw that his pee color had lightened up to almost normal.

Culligan returned to the front of the sand dune and again looked out to sea. He shook his head, and laughing, he said, "Larco has them coming about and doing figure eights!"

Cassy looked at him puzzled. Culligan traced out a figure eight in the sand and Cassy nodded that she understood.

• • •

Larco and Culligan were lazing under Grandfather Oak, Cassy was off some distance, when Preacher Sorenson from the Baptist Church came to visit. He said, "This is a religious community, and you two men have not seen fit to visit our church. That, along with you taking up with a colored, has raises questions. There are some in this County, like Bobby Felton and Uncle Josh, who are grateful for what you have brought to this corner of the world, but this is a land has suffered a great defeat, and you two taking up with a colored, is rubbing our nose in it. Doing for this colored girl, with most whites being so poor, is a bitterness that could boil over any-minute. I would not like to see a member of my congregation commit an act that would endanger their immortal soul—plus you are well-armed, and I am told you are a good man with a gun. Are you well enough to travel?"

"Soon, but not yet."

• • •

Uncle Josh echoed, "Culligan, I appreciate the business you provide but after you've been properly outfitted and feel stronger, you need to move on. I see there are times when you need to be alone. Still, you have taken on caring for your little colored girl."

Culligan looked up. "Josh, is this leading somewhere?"

Josh's face paled. Swallowing, he said, "It is. You are not the kind to show off—but when you laid that twenty dollar gold piece on my counter I knew right off that you had money. Now everyone knows.

"You are not a sociable man Mister Culligan. Eventually you will grow tired and snappy with caring for Cassy. Your friend Larco is the most easy to like man I ever met, more so than Cal, the husband my sister had, and a better man than Cal ever thought of being. So, if you and Larco head out west, and taking Cassy with you, and if Larco gets set up with a way to provide for my sister, then I will provide my sister with the means to go to him. My sister has no children and neither does Larco. They could care for Cassy those times when you feel the need to get away."

Culligan stood still. His look caused Uncle Josh to swallow. Then Culligan said, "Josh, you are one smart storekeeper."

• • •

Uncle Josh was able to outfit Cassy with a split skirt in strong linen, boots, practical undergarments, a broad-brimmed hat and a practical coat.

Culligan said, "Larco, you about ready to head out west with me and Cassy?"

"For damn sure there is no way I will be going back to sea."

Culligan nodded, "That was my first shipwreck and that one time is more than enough. While you were off courting Hetty, I promised Cassy I would teach her to ride and shoot and otherwise take care of herself.

But a white man traveling alone with a black girl—he can expect some trouble. You being a stand-up man, and with that Winchester and the Derringer you took off the dead Affleck brother—us riding together and watching each other's backs—maybe then I won't have to be killing anyone. I done enough of that already."

"With you, me, and Cassy partnered up," Culligan continued, "my having money in banks in Vancouver BC, and Sacramento, more than I can ever spend, then I could give each of you twenty dollars a month and you could teach Cassy how to count with numbers and add and subtract with money."

Larco's reply went right to the point. "That would allow me to give what I already have to Hetty. I want to keep her thinking of me."

"Decent mounts for the three of us are part of the expense and I'll be picking that up."

• • •

Samuel Woodson was 6 foot 2 inches tall, hollow-eyed, and a skeletal 170 pounds. He drove his buckboard into Belting and saw Cassy and Larco walking along and laughing together. Her walking along with a white man was insulting enough. Then seeing what she was wearing enraged him. He jumped off the buckboard and rushed towards Cassy. Larco stepped in front of her and with the Derringer under his hand. Samuel's feet skidded to a stop and the thunder in his voice said, "Them's my dead girl's boots and that nigger gal has no call to be wearing them!"

"She has the right! You sold them to Uncle Josh and Culligan bought them for Cassy so she has the right!"

Samuel's eyes turned back to his shotgun leaning against the seat of his buckboard.

Culligan walked up, with his right thumb he raised up his loose shirt and that put his hand on the Remington Avenging Angel.

Samuel backed down, and sick with rage, climbed up on his buckboard and pulled away.

"So many in this land," Culligan said, "look like that man. Having a few days of not eating never hurt anyone, but years of not ever having a full belly. . . it leaves a mark on a man."

Word went out about what happened. Some grumbled that maybe they should do something about it; some said they should mind their own business.

"Still," Culligan said, "It only takes one."

Larco nodded. "How did guns with short barrels like yours get known as Avenging Angels?"

"Orrin Porter Rockwell, known as the Mormon Avenging Angel, had been the first to saw off the barrel of his handgun and was known to have killed 28 men and was suspected of having killed more. He was in process of being tried for murder when he died of natural causes. From that time on handguns with sawed off barrels were known as Avenging Angels. My bellygun is cut down to a three inch barrel and with a dovetail front sight."

• • •

They had been in Belting too long. The town had initially been sympathetic to the plight of the shipwreck survivors but the town was poor, shamed by having lost the war, had lost many of its young, and some not so young men, and now seeing that outsiders had so much more than them, even that little colored girl now being well off, there were dark grumblings.

Uncle Josh and the liveryman looked about for three riding horses and a pack animal. For himself, Culligan purchased the big gray gelding that the liveryman located. A decent looking and gentled down brown mare suited Larco just fine. Finding a mount that was right for Cassy took some time.

Culligan rode into Belting leading a young saddle pony. For the moment, the looks that had scared Cassy in previous days were forgotten. She dared not hope—yet she fell in love with that pony the moment she laid eyes on him. "For me?"

Culligan nodded and said, "For you."

He sat her up in the saddle and adjusted the stirrups to the right length. "Your pony's name is Chico. Why they gave Chico a Spanish name I don't know, but anyway."

Cassy was about as happy as a young girl could ever be. They rode out of town for an hour . . . then back to the livery stable, unsaddled their mounts and pack mule, gave them rubdowns, put them in stalls, hayed and grained them while Cassy paid close attention on how to rub down, grain, and settle her pony. Cassy still jumped to obey any directive from either of the men, but now, it was with dragging feet that Cassy walked away from spending the night in the stall with Chico.

The next day was spent gathering rice, beans, corn meal, dried vegetable mix, and coffee. Culligan also purchased oil slickers and bedrolls.

On a cool, still, morning and with the sun not yet risen, with the air still and not a cloud in the sky, the supplies were loaded on the pack mule and Culligan, Larco, and Cassy saddled up.

Culligan and Cassy sat their horses at some distance away while Larco and Hetty Baldwin said their goodbyes. Then, as ready as they could ever be, the three friends began their westward journey.

• • •

Years later, Larco said, "Hetty, travel that first day meant riding for an hour, dismounting, and then walking our horses for another hour. For an old seaman, that was way different from what I had known. I was a seaman, not much of a walker on land and not yet much of a horseman."

Before noon, they came across a small nook that had sparkling water, green grass, and bushes and trees that were in flower. They gave the horses and pack mule a rubdown and tethered them in good graze.

After the noon meal Culligan said, "Cassy, what say you and I go fishing while Larco keeps an eye on things at camp?"

They had fish and cornbread for their evening meal.

• • •

On the afternoon of their second day in Georgia, Larco said, "I remember from when I was a boy. That fresh damp smell in the wind says that a storm's on the way." They set up the tent and pickets were driven down hard.

The storm broke with rolling thunder and sheets of rain. First came hard, wind-driven drops, then came a cloud of needle-sharp hail and jagged forks of lightening filled the air. The three of them crowded into the small tent. Larco sang out a sea chantey and taught Cassy how to sing the chorus part. Cassy felt safe.

"Cully," Larco said, "You run into this kind of weather on the Oregon Trail?"

"I never slipped and slid around in red clay like now, and I never ran into swamps and piney woods like these, and the air smelled a whole lot different, but I have seen lots worse weather than this. One day on the Platte River there was a distant rumbling of thunder. The usual warning of a coming thunderstorm was the gathering of dark clouds and rolling thunder. I was on the North side of the Platte. I took the usual cautions to meet the storm and watched for the flashes of lightening that heralded such storms, but there were none. That cloud was on the south side of the Platte and seemed to be heading directly at me, was growing louder, nearer, and was different in color than was usual. Then the ground trembled. When the dust lifted I saw a black mass of buffalo, a tight-packed herd more than a mile long and I don't know how wide came thundering by.

"I be damned. You ever see anything like that again Cully?"

"Never did. I had been on the south side of the Platte the day before and on this day I was real glad to be on the north side. Sometimes I saw smaller herds of two or three buffalo and sometimes one alone but mostly the lonesome ones were so old and spavined that they were only bone and gristle. I ate buffalo only twice in over a 1,000 miles but I did eat a lot of antelope."

• • •

Larco could read, write, and spell but not well. Riding into Georgia, each day he wrote something for Hetty Baldwin, and each day he would ask Culligan for the proper spelling of several of the words. Laboring in this way, in ten days he had a letter ready to send.

Dear Hetty,
Well here we are. Each day Culligan, Cassy and me, we get up before dawn, eat, break camp, and ride out. At around midday, when we find a spot that offers good graze and fresh water, we stop for the day. Sometimes we ride into towns and grain our horses and stable them for the night. The next day, at dawn, we ride out. Each passing day, me and Culligan recover some of the strength and weight we lost in that lifeboat. Also, Cassy's head is being held high and now she looks each of us in the eye.
Skinny little Cassy sure can eat. It appears that all three of us had gone hungry for some time.

Cassy pays constant attention to her horse Chico. Also the morning, noon, and evening meals sure do get her attention. Traveling together and while on horseback I teach Cassy to recite the alphabet. There are sounds in some of the letters that Cassy has never used. The letter R was real hard for her but she has learned to speak every letter of the alphabet. When we were in Belting, Cassy sometimes spoke a language that me and Culligan did not understand. Uncle Josh told us that the language was called Gullah. When we make camp I scratch out letters in the dirt for Cassy.

Hetty, I think of you every day and night. When the day comes when I know I can provide for you then I will ask for your hand.

Larco

Chapter Three—Living on the edge

In Washington DC, in the Spring of 1858, Serena McNabb, had entered the War Office. A secretary referred her to Captain Kellogg. Captain Kellogg was near-sighted, overweight, and not as tall as Serena. Her first impression was that Captain Kellogg was an ordinary man.

Then, Serena took a second look. She said, "Insurrection is in the air and I am requesting employment as a spy. I request that I be commissioned to journey into Southern States where I may ferret out information pertaining to the impending conflict."

"Uh huh. Spies are executed when caught. Why would you put yourself at such risk?

"Money could be a reason."

"Usually, criminals, cutthroats, and prostitutes are preferred for this kind of work. Do you have you this kind of experience?"

Calmly, she said, "I do not."

"Have you offered your services to the South?"

"I have not and I will not! There can be no question. The North has the industrial power. Ultimately, the North will prevail. Any moneys I received from the South, unless it was in gold or silver coin, would be worthless at war's end. I prefer being on the winning side."

"Is being on the winning side your goal?"

"I recognize it is unwise to reveal more than is needed. Still, I admit that I deplore slavery. My hope is that with the war's end, slavery in this country will be abolished."

"What," Captain Kellogg said, "have you told them at the front desk?"

"I said I wanted to talk with someone because I have information that may be useful."

"At the front desk . . . did you give them your name?"

"I gave the name of a total stranger."

Captain Kellogg nodded, pushed a pen and paper across to her saying, "Write down your name and address."

Captain Kellogg drummed his fingers on his desk while she wrote. She pushed the paper over to him.

"My secretary," he said, "has a loose tongue. So you will leave my Office looking stiff-necked and in a huff. I will be coming behind you while staring at the floor and shaking my head. I will meet with you at your residence at 8PM and then we will talk."

• • •

Captain Kellogg arrived at Serena McNabb's door. He gave two quick knocks and the door opened. He entered, removed his derby hat, wiped his sweating brow, and sat. She remained standing.

Captain Kellogg looked off into space. Then he stared at Serena. "Tell me about you."

"The family fortune came from the slave trade. That troubled me. My brother Jonathan berated me for my lack of appreciation for all the good that came out of the slave trade. Stuart reminded me that it was the slave trade that provided our family with our gracious manner of living."

"Evidently," Captain Kellogg said, "you do not always hide what you think."

"I hid my rebellious thoughts and feelings for seventeen years. I've had a lot of practice at that, but then I cut the family umbilical cord. When I commented on how the men in the family all hide behind a mask of piety, my father said: 'Young lady, I am a deacon of the church and do not impugn my standing in the church!'

"I will admit Father, that in social gatherings, you miss few opportunities to quote from Scripture."

"You need to return to Scripture," father bellowed, "and away from that French rubbish that has turned you away from the true path to salvation!"

Captain Kellogg nodded. "I can understand your need to get away. Was there ever a man in your life?"

"I was seventeen years old when Sir John Knowles, a middle aged, widowed, wealthy, and distant cousin to the Crown, expressed an interest in me. My parents saw this as a family coupe and began making arrangements for my marriage to Sir John."

"What did you do?"

"I declared, 'I am not going to share a marriage bed with Sir John! That is something I would not enjoy, and I will not do it!'"

"And what was their response?"

"My father and two brothers began berating me while mother, who otherwise never spoke up, intervened. She said that they should respect the rights of two women to discuss this matter in private. She said: 'If you will allow, Serena will join with me in the next room for a womanly talk.'"

"And?"

"Once alone, Mother whispered that it would be scandalous if others were to hear that I expected to 'enjoy' the marriage bed, that no lady could ever enjoy such activities, and that only an animal or a harlot would take pleasure in engaging in such acts.

"I said, why do it if you don't enjoy it?"

"It was my wifely duty," Mother said, "and I can say with pride that I have never enjoyed even one second of such activities."

"How sad. Your pride has the ring of pomposity to it. There must be a better name for this but I don't know what it could be."

"My father was outraged. He said: Either you marry Sir John or you will be placed in a Convent!"

Captain Kellogg lifted his eyes and said, "What then?"

"My family heaved a sigh of relief when I agreed to marry Sir John."

"And did you marry him?"

"What I did was take the money allotted for my wedding dress and booked passage on a steamship bound for New York City. The call for Insurrection was being heard even in England. I took a position teaching small children while honing my skills as a writer. Now, insurrection is eminent. While War is a terrible thing for the many, for the few, there is profit. The conflict offers me a challenge, offers me financial gain, plus material for the career I intend as a writer."

• • •

Serena McNabb was the youngest spy Captain Kellogg ever hired, she journeyed into southern states, and labored, under the byline of S. McNabb, as a freelance writer of short stories, poetry, and theatre reviews.

When the War for the Confederacy broke out, she visited hospitals, other locations, and churned out many a heart-rending account of how the brave young men of the Confederacy were coping.

Sitting at a restaurant window with a pot of tea, Serena could observe everything, including the number of columns, the number of cannon, types of armament, all while simultaneously writing poetry. A Confederate Officer looked over her shoulder to determine what Serena was writing. She looked up and said, "Yes?"

"Forgive me. Now I see that you are writing a theater review and not about military matters."

"You are forgiven Colonel."

"Colonel Elkins." He looked in her eyes. Were they gray, green, or gray/green? He felt a need to explain his position—his responsibilities—and did so—.

• • •

Serena dispatched information by courier. When she was unsure about what information might be of value, she would let those in the Confederate Military decide by writing it up as a newspaper article, and the editors would omit certain parts. Confederate Officers were helpful as they informed the editors of what material to cut. Serena would take note of what had been omitted and send that material north.

• • •

Serena recognized the eventual dawn of suspicion in the eye of Confederate Officer Captain Small who had already lost his left eye and right arm. Though damaged, he was still an officer to be reckoned with.

The sky was clear and the stars overhead shone like diamonds as Serena rode sidesaddle out into the night.

At a later date, Serena was to admit, "I had become addicted to living on the edge. In the nick of time I recognized that I had gone too far. I flew away—Later I learned that I had narrowly escaped those sent to arrest me."

Serena avoided pitched battles but the smoke of burnt powder and the look and stench of dead bodies was less easily avoided. Isolated soldiers, both Union and Confederate, were helpful in providing Serena with information that allowed her to avoid troop movements. The sounds of pitched battles were sometimes at hand but she was able to pass around both Confederate and Union lines unscathed.

• • •

Captain Kellogg's success at gleaning intelligence had not gone unnoticed. On Serena's return to Washington, she reported to now Colonel Kellogg. He said, "You took chances."

"Too many. Succeeding in dangerous undertakings triggered an unrealistic conviction that I would not get caught.

Kellogg nodded, "You came close."

She nodded, "I went too far. I have personally experienced both the fear of discovery and the subsequent exhilaration in not being discovered. Something you said when we first met, you said your secretary had a loose tongue."

"He did, and that proved useful. I used him as fish bait, watched those who courted his attention, watched when they swallowed the hook, and then we reeled them in."

Staring out his window at the Potomac, Major Kellogg said, "Would you be willing to continue on the Federal payroll and help me ferret out spies in the North?"

"I would."

• • •

Serena played a significant role in the recognition and the breaking up of a link in the conduit that fed information to the

Confederacy.

"Serena," Colonel Kellogg said, "you are the most reliable and the best agent I ever had. Sherman's successful march to the sea has assured Lincoln's reelection and already foretold, finally, our inevitable victory. But, politics being politics, I must inform you that your Federal Employment is now at an end."

Nodding, Serena said, "I saw it coming."

"You have plans?"

"Eventually, I hope to return to England as an established writer. Thanks to my Federal Employment I now have money, but I will require additional funds as I intend to return to England in style and establish myself as a writer in my homeland."

"What about marriage, having children?"

"Maybe someday."

Chapter Four—A gunfight

Early Fall in Georgia, and with Larco stretched out on his bed-roll, he said, "Cully, how did you come to walk across the Isthmus and set sail on the Starling?"

"You smell those wild onions in the air?"

"Sure do. Myself" Larco said, "I shipped in and out of Panama three times and once even went for a walk in the jungle. The closeness of things and the sound of insects is what I remember most. To tell the truth, I was more comfortable in a seaport saloon. "

Culligan nodded. "After all the harshness, all the cold, and all the quiet I had heard for three years up in British Columbia, I relished the lushness of the foliage and the sightings and sounds of the birds. I was in no hurry but my stride ate up the miles. One morning I saw a tree smothered in butterflies. Then the butterflies, thousands of them, as if of one mind, all rose up in the air and flew south; that cloud of butterflies flowing south was a wonderous sight."

"Did the jungle sort of crowd in on you?"

"After a time it did. At one village I met a woman who pointed out the path that led up to the top of the mountain and from there, she said, I would be able to see both the Atlantic and Pacific Oceans, both from the same spot. Walking up that path I thought, *that middle-aged woman is too friendly and smiling too much.* So, on the way up, I took note of the good spots from which to ambush.

One spot was perfect. Up ahead there was a ridge of bare rock to hide behind. I worked my way up behind that ridge, searched the ground, and sure enough, I found spent shells."

"So what did you do?"

"I got back on the path and climbed the mountain. The skies were clear that day and I could see both the Pacific and the Atlantic from that spot. So, coming down, about a 100 yards before I reached the ambush spot, I cut off the path and worked my way up behind that ridge. Sure enough, a man was lying there and waiting. He heard me chamber a cartridge and tried to jump to the other side of that ridge."

"He make it?"

"He did not. Lifting and moving a dead body is hard work and he was a fat one. I dragged him off about fifty yards and dropped him and his rifle over a ledge . . . saw skeletons down where I dropped him.

"Coming down, I saw the woman waiting and thanked her for telling me about the view. She smiled her way through her confusion."

• • •

Cassy asked Larco, "How do you know Cully?"

"I had signed onto the ship Starling, and then Culligan walked into Colon, that's in Panama, a country way south of here. He came aboard, and booked passage. We were set to sail for Baltimore on the morning tide, and none too soon. The air was hot, muggy, and barely moving.

"First Mate Deke Webster and I had watched as Culligan came aboard. He paid for his passage and stowed his Spenser, bedroll and backpack on his bunk and then he left the ship. I said to Deke that the way Culligan's clothes looked I bet he walked all the way across the Isthmus."

Nodding, First Mate Deke Webster, said, "The suit he's wearing was a good suite once. He probably needed to save his money to book passage."

• • •

Culligan, on leaving the ship, purchased a clean set of clothes, visited the barbershop, showered, changed into new clothes, not as good quality as the previous suit had been, but clean and undamaged, and climbed into the barber chair for a haircut and beard trim while also getting a boot shine. He left the dirty clothes for whoever wanted them.

The only clothing he had kept were his belt, boots and hat. The waterproof money belt under his shirt held Gold Certificates and large denomination bills. Gold and silver coins were carried in his pockets.

Feeling like a new man, Culligan entered a fine restaurant.

• • •

When Culligan returned to the ship, First Mate Deke Webster said, "You coming back aboard . . . you sure don't look much like the same man went ashore."

Agreeably, Culligan said, "Don't much feel like him either."

Entering the cabin, he stretched out on his bunk. The two other passengers were the brothers Floyd and Ralph Affleck. Culligan remembered them from when he was a boy in the gold camp up on the Rosebud and he knew they were now wanted in California for robbery/ murder. They introduced themselves as the Bishop Brothers. Culligan nodded and accepted that even though they all recognized each other. In the past, Culligan had liked the Affleck brothers—and, as the Bishop Brothers, he liked them now—but them now being wanted for robbery/murder in California, things were touchy.

• • •

When Culligan was a boy back in New York City, his mother had said: "With the money I saved, plus the money you bring in selling newspapers and selling the fish you catch, Springtime, we'll travel by train to St. Louis and travel in a wagon train to Oregon. I'll marry a decent man, and we'll start a new life."

Then Culligan's mother was murdered.

• • •

Able-Bodied-Seaman Larco was about five foot six inches tall and about 140 pounds. Larco wasn't sure, but he thought he might be 42 years old. He was a cheerful sort of a man and Culligan recognized that even the younger and bigger seamen were hard-pressed to keep up with Larco—none could climb up through the rigging like Larco.

Larco noted Culligan spent much of his time on deck and said, "I see you checking out the waves and sails for which way the true wind is blowing."

Culligan nodded. "Trying to make sense of it."

Larco didn't ask many questions, but he was sociable sort and willing to do the talking if others were of a mind to listen. One time he said, "They tell me that as an infant, I was left on the steps of an orphanage in Baltimore. Who my parents were and how I got handed the name Larco was never explained to me. If I ever had a second name I sure never heard it. Maybe Larco was my second name. At age about twelve I was turned over to a chicken farmer. That son-of-a-bitch worked me hard. I must have been about fifteen when I stole the farmer's Barlow knife and stowed away aboard a ship leaving port on the morning tide. I served aboard that ship with half pay for a year before signing up on a whaling ship out of Nantucket. On that whaling ship it was usually me who was the one to shout, 'Thar she blows!' I had the best eyes on the ship."

Culligan was less easily forthcoming, but admitted, "I went by one name too. And my eyesight has always been good. In any company of men, I always seem to be the best shot."

"Uh huh." Larco said, "You always carry a gun?"

"I do. My mother had been well-acquainted with Walt Fipps. He was a good burglar. Walt sold Mom a maple case housing two five-shot Colts in 36 caliber. The triggers were housed in the spur and popped up when the hammer was pulled down. Those Colts were handsome, nickel-plated, and had ivory grips."

"New York treated my mother bad, then it killed her. So, after my mother's funeral, I packed up and took the Colts, the jar money mother and I had saved, our hatchet, made up a bedroll, took a ferry across the Hudson, and from there I started walking westward."

"How old were you?"

"I was fourteen. That Spring, Summer, and Fall I worked for a dairy farmer for room, board, and damn little pay. Winter time the farmer let me go."

"Uh huh. By different routes, both of us ended up on our own at an early age and each of us with only the one name."

Larco was talkative but he noticed that Culligan would fill up with too much talk and walk away.

Larco took no offense.

• • •

The Starling sailed from Colon in fair weather. They had cleared the Caribbean when all hell broke loose. Larco said, "Even sailing around the Horn I never saw it this bad!" The ship Starling was taking a beating and springing leaks in all its pores.

Culligan and the Bishop Brothers heaved-to manning the pumps while Rendel and Isler, the two passengers in the other cabin, offered no help. The storm abated some, but still, one piece at a time, the Starling continued to founder and fall apart. After two days of calmer seas and wind, and about midway between Africa and the Americas, the men abandoned ship . . . and none too soon.

While aboard ship, Culligan had been drinking as much water as he could keep down, he had also dumped the brandy out of his small flask and filled it with water. He carried the short-barreled Avenging Angel in his waistband holster and the flask, plus caps and balls, a powder flask, a tin of grease he called bearshit, because it looked like bear shit, plus a preloaded cylinder, in his vest pockets. At dawn they lowered three lifeboats into the still roiling sea. Culligan and Larco, along with the Bishop brothers, Rendel and Isler, entered the smallest lifeboat. First Mate Deke Webster took the tiller, oars were manned, and the seamen pulled away from the ship. Once free of possible undertow, they shipped oars and raised sail.

First mate Deke Webster was a strong and able seaman, but he was also a heavy drinker, had just come off a month-long drunk, and the rains did him in. He became too ill to do anything but lie shivering in the bottom of the boat.

Larco and Slaby took over the tiller. Clearly, they were capable . . . plus, Larco had been through shipwreck before.

The Bishop Brothers and Culligan sat in the bottom of the boat, butts in inches of water, and bailed.

On the twelfth day Deke Webster died. Prayers were offered up and Webster was returned to the sea.

On the sixteenth day the rains stopped and the skies grew free of clouds.

It got hot.

On the twenty-third day in the lifeboat, Culligan recognized that the Bishop brothers were distancing themselves. Ralph said, "Culligan, like when we were aboard ship, we see you watching how sail is managed. If push came to shove, you think you could handle that tiller and sail?"

"Probably could."

Rendel and Isler were in the bow, unarmed, and useless as barnacles.

Coming across a patch of seaweed, Larco had them lift the seaweed aboard. Shrimp flopped out of the seaweed. They baited two lines with a shrimp and dropped then over the side. The rest of the shrimp were devoured.

The raw flesh of fish provided them with a hint of moisture and some nourishment. Evening, when the air cooled, they received their ration of water.

On the twenty-sixth day, the Bishop Brothers huddled. Looking to Culligan they said, "You with us?"

"No." Three shots were fired. Culligan's two shots took out the Bishop Brothers while their one shot went high.

Like Culligan, the Bishop Brother's had money belts under their shirts. Culligan said, "In California them two were known as the Affleck Brothers and were wanted for robbery and murder. The money in those belts is blood money."

Seamen are generally superstitious. Slaby, along with Larco, decided they already had enough bad luck, and wanted nothing to do with blood money. Rendel and Isler took the Affleck Brother's money belts and Navy Colts, while Larco laid claim to Floyd Affleck's Derringer.

The bodies of Floyd and Ralph Affleck were dumped overboard. Good riddance and more water for the rest of them.

• • •

They were now down to five.

Larco and Slaby were the only helmsmen. When Slaby was relieved, he took his seat next to the keel housing, his eyes rolled up, and he slumped over dead.

Prayers were said for his Deliverance and Slaby, a decent man, was reverently assigned to the deep. Now they were four.

• • •

No way could Larco continue as the only helmsman. Culligan's management of the helm did not measure up to the standards of Larco, and they lost some speed, but there was little luffing of the sail and he did keep them heading westward.

On the 28th day they saw rain squalls to the North and South of their position but none overhead. They looked yearningly at those rain squalls and prayed for a visit by the rain, but the skies overhead remained hot and clear and offered not a hint of water.

That night, dehydrated, exhausted, and on the point of death, for the first time, Culligan broke out his water flask, drank it all, and lived through the night. Shortly before dawn they smelled land. Dawn light revealed land was at hand.

• • •

Culligan had been hearing and seeing things he knew were not there yet he welcomed the hearing of his mother's voice. Now he thought he could hear the sound of waves lapping on the shore but he wasn't sure—like his mother's voice—what if it was only a dream? When the bow of the boat crunched up on the sandy shore and jarred his back, Culligan knew it was real.

• • •

The girl on shore thought that men in such a desperate condition might have little interest in harming her. Still, you could never tell about white men.

Years later Culligan would say to Serena McNabb, "When that girl looked me in my eyes, I knew there was no escape; I was tied to that girl. I looked in her eyes and recognized myself in her, the fourteen year old who had lost his mother and not ever having known a father. I was surprised seeing myself in this skinny young black girl but there it was. I think that when she looked in my eyes she must

38

have seen herself in the boy I had been after losing my mother."

Chapter Five— Meet Earl Bates Sr.

Serena had moved to Philadelphia. As a freelance writer she churned out theater and book reviews, poetry, and human interest stories. At a later date she stated, "I wrote out everything but restaurant menus."

• • •

This had not been the best of days. Eighteen months had passed since her Federal Employment had ended, and this day Serena McNabb had sold none of her stories and none of her poems. Plus, the streets and roads were clogged with snow and ice and a chill wind was blowing.

So, in the gathering gloom, she abandoned the snow-choked streets of Philadelphia for her hotel. Her entrance signaled the desk clerk, like the peacock he was, to strut and preen his flowing mustaches. He was pleased to see her fatigue, it made her more vulnerable and so he greeted this potential trophy with his most winning smile.

Calmly, Serena commanded, "My key please."

The desk clerk handed her the key from her key box.

"And the letter from my key box. That will save both of us the trouble of you having to come knocking on my door while I am getting settled."

Moving to the warmth of the lobby stove, she removed her

gloves, slapped her hands together and stamped her frozen feet. This day had been the culmination of a week of perfectly rotten days. She opened the letter.

Dear Miss McNabb,
Colonel Kellogg has spoken highly of your resourcefulness during the War. I wish to interview you pertaining to possible employment. Enclosed you will find a voucher for 50 dollars. As soon as your affairs will allow, use these monies to contact me at the Boston Office of Bates, Bates, & Collier.
Yours truly,
Earl Bates Sr.

Serena was being paid only a penny a line for her poetry and the voucher for $50 was a godsend. Once more she had escaped the need to draw from her wartime savings.

• • •

Early on a bitterly cold January morning, Serena provided herself with comfortable transportation to the city of Boston. She leaned back on the train cushions. It occurred to her that when you are feeling tired, hungry, or needy, you don't get the job. *Never beg and never look needy.* Only someone she did not choose to work for would hire a beggar.

It occurred to Serena that no matter how well dressed she might be, if her stomach was empty Mr. Earl Bates would sense something was not right, and she would not get the job. *If my stomach is full,* she thought, *he will sense that as well.* Whether my stomach is full of steak or full of beans probably will not matter, but let us not take chances.

On arrival in Boston, in order to provide herself with the proper frame of mind, Serena checked into a respectable hotel for the night. The following morning she treated herself to a sumptuous breakfast. Ready then, with calmness of mind and under an overcast sky, she hired a carriage to deliver her to the offices of Bates, Bates, & Collier.

Presenting herself at the front office, she said to the secretary, "My name is Miss Serena McNabb, and I request an audience with

Mister Earl Bates Senior."

The secretary entered the office of Earl Bates Senior. He returned and informed her, "Mr. Bates will see you now."

Earl Bates met Serena at the door, ushered her to a chair and said to his secretary, "Please provide Miss McNabb with a pot of tea."

Returning to his desk, he said, "Your arrival at this time is most salutary. Allow me to finish with these reports. Then I will be with you."

Serena took the time to scrutinize Earl Bates Sr. He appeared to be in his fifties or early sixties. A good figure of a man, but with a sallow complexion that indicated he was not well. Serena was familiar with the look; having seen it in wounded soldiers. Some lingered, some recovered, some did not.

The secretary arrived with a pot of tea and waited while Bates Sr. finished the last of the reports. When the secretary left with the reports, Earl Bates leaned back in his chair and scrutinized Serena.

"You have been described to me as courageous and resourceful. I am told that under your calm and genteel exterior, you have nerves of steel and that in the late insurrection you served as a spy from deep within Southern territories. According to Colonel Kellogg you also became one of the most successful of those employed to ferret out spies in the North. I find this remarkable.

"There is also a rumor that you come from a prominent English family and either you disowned them or they disowned you. Would you care to explain?"

"I would not. I must tell you that I find your suggestion that I explain myself impertinent! You did not send for me to discuss my private life, my conduct, or that of my family."

Earl Bates was silent and in thought. He cleared his throat to speak only to be interrupted by Serena who said, "I will tell you this much. You asked about what happened in my family. Why? That question suggests that family matters are on your mind, possibly relating to your own family, and you may be curious to see if my family issues bear any resemblance to your family issues."

Earl Bates reared back, went to the window, paused and stated, "I am not the only one being impertinent. I think I understand why, despite your obvious intelligence, you might have difficulty maintaining employment. You probably scare the bejabbers out of people."

Snow was falling.

Mister Earl Bates returned to his desk. Looking up, he said, "You are, of course . . . quite right," then he slumped into his chair. Rousing his self, he sat erect and continued, "I had no intention of revealing this but you have opened the gates. When I was young, I was courting Nancy Borden. She was beautiful and, I thought, a decent enough young woman. Her family and my family were intent that the two of us were to marry. Then, on a visit to my parent's home I met Mary Culligan. Mary was a young Irish immigrant employed as a chambermaid in my parent's home. It was obvious to everyone that I was smitten with Mary and she with me. My parents and Nancy Borden were flabbergasted. Nancy was far the more beautiful, but Mary Culligan had that spirit, that vitality . . . that something.

"The short time I had with Mary Culligan was the brightest time of my life. She was so energetic, so alive. To me, she was the truest person in the world. A poor immigrant girl, Mary had taught herself to read and write, loved books, theatre, and long walks. I had a scheduled business trip and told Mary that on my return I would have something to tell her. It was my intention, on my return, to propose to Mary. Yet on my return Mary was not to be seen. I asked mother, 'Where's Mary?' My mother hesitated before admitting, 'Mary's gone.'

"Haltingly, my mother informed me that Mary had left in the company of a wealthy older gentleman. In a voice that attempted to comfort me, my mother explained that although I had been fond of Mary, the truth was that Mary was only another poor girl looking for a rich husband. My mother had never lied to me. Fool that I was I accepted my mother's explanation—it was not my finest hour—and I was never the same after that.

"Even though my heart wasn't in it, I married Nancy Borden. Years later I discovered that during my absence, my parents and Nancy Borden, conspiring together, staged a little scene for Mary's benefit . . . where they discussed arrangements for the upcoming marriage between myself and Nancy Borden.

"That little scene, staged for Mary's benefit, convinced Mary that I had proposed to Nancy and we were to be married on my return.

"Then, after having convinced Mary that I had only been trifling with her, my parents informed Mary that her employment would need to be terminated as her presence would tempt my attentions to wander. They provided Mary with a month's extra pay, fourteen dollars, to leave Boston and never return.

"I married Nancy Borden and have three children by her, an unmarried son and two married daughters. After my youngest daughter's birth my wife developed a high fever and became delirious. Thinking that she was talking to my mother, Nancy relived their plot to disillusion and discredit Mary Culligan. When she recovered from her fever I confronted my wife with what she had inadvertently revealed. Both my wife and my mother were unrepentant and proclaimed that what they had done had been for my own good and that I should be grateful!"

"I have not spoken to my wife or my parents since that day. My parents have now passed on.

"When I learned the truth, I hired Pinkerton Detectives to look for Mary Culligan. I learned that Mary had traveled to New York where she delivered a child she named William Culligan. I thought it probable that he was my son."

Earl Bates bowed his head and appeared unable to speak. The moment passed. He recovered himself and continued, "At the time I began my inquiries, a number of prostitutes in New York had been found with their throats cut. Mary Culligan was one of those unfortunates."

Earl Bates was again overcome. Gathering himself, he continued, "Mary Culligan's child simply disappeared. The Pinkertons could find no trace of him."

"I was at my Club when I chanced to hear a buyer from California regaling his host with the exploits of a lumberjack. The gentleman from California told the tale of this man Culligan who, after years of prospecting with little success, turned to work as a lumberjack. On his last year as a lumberjack, he worked as a tree topper. Topping trees consists of working one's way up the trunk of a tall tree and then topping off the top of the tree. When the top of the tree falls free the main trunk, now free of leaf and limb, will swing back and forth while the tree-topper hangs on for dear life."

On one of those occasions, as Culligan rode the trunk swinging back and forth, he caught a glimpse of where the nearby small stream dropped over a ledge and into a pool. The stream then hurried on.

After they were clear of the area, he quit the crew, returned alone, built a sluice box and worked that pool for gold. Reports are that he worked that pool for $500 in gold, more than he would make in a year as a lumberjack.

"I learned," Earl Bates said, "that the gentleman in question did not acknowledge having a first name.

"Again, I hired Pinkertons. They confirmed the existence out West, at various times and at various locations, of this man Culligan, but were unable to establish his present location, only where he had been."

Earl Bates paused. Then, shaking with heaviness, he continued, "I need you to locate this man. Recent developments have confirmed that he is indeed my son. This man Culligan is all that's left of the great love of my life. I want Mary Culligan's son to know how sorry I am, how much I loved her."

For a time, Earl Bates was lost in reminiscence. "I am told that Culligan is a big man and something of a loner. He worked sometimes as a logger and more often as a prospector. He struck it rich in British Columbia—has substantial deposits in banks in Vancouver BC and in Sacramento. He is now wealthy and yet, according to all I have learned, he continues living out in the open most of the year. Apparently, it is only with the return of cold weather that he returns to the comforts of a town.

"He is a reader, and in his travels, he carries Shakespeare. One informant stated that Culligan once stated that if he were to settle anywhere it would probably be in East Africa or Australia or any other land that offered open space and warm weather year around."

Earl Bates continued, "Recently, after having written to you, I received a report from one of the Pinkertons originally involved in the search for Mary Culligan. He had kept tabs on William Culligan's old neighborhood and on Mary Culligan's gravesite. He no longer worked for the Pinkerton's and his information was for sale.

"I learned that William Culligan had returned to New York and visited the grave of his mother. The Sexton reported that observing from his office window, he saw this man Culligan stand at Mary Culligan's grave on a bitterly cold and windy day for nearly three hours.

"Upon Culligan's leaving, the Sexton was unable to resist asking Culligan what he had been doing all that time out there in the cold? Culligan replied that he had been telling his mother all that had happened since they last talked."

• • •

On leaving his mother's grave, Culligan paid a visit to the area along the docks of New York's West Side. His ferry to Fort Lee would not be leaving till late afternoon. So, with his suitcase and riflecase he dropped into Murphy's Bar. He spent most of the afternoon pounding down one drink after another.

Eddy was tending bar. Eddy is a big man, which is needed if you tend bar in that rough part of town, and while Culligan remembered Eddy from their childhood, Eddy did not recognize him. Culligan did not drink often but when he did there were times when he drank a lot. This was one of those times. Eddy expected trouble the way Culligan was pounding down the drinks but that never happened. Culligan minded his own business and liquor didn't seem to rattle his brain. Late that afternoon, with a belly full of booze and yet still steady on his feet, he looked at his timepiece and asked if old man Murphy still owned the bar?

Surprised, Eddy responded, "Old man Murphy's been dead almost ten years! His son owns the bar now."

"Huh. Artie owns the bar now."

Hearing this Eddy said, "I've been here all my life and I thought I knew everyone in the neighborhood. Do I know you?"

Tossing down his drink, Culligan picked up his suitcase and rifle case and said, "You ought to know me Eddy. It was me whipped your ass when we were kids." Then he turned and walked out the door.

Eddy came out from behind the bar and looked after Culligan, who was headed down the walkway to the ferry dock. Artie, the bar's owner, arrived in time to hear Eddy exclaim, "I just now realized who that is! That's Willy Culligan!"

"The hell you say!" Artie rushed after Culligan shouting, "Hey Willy, Willy Culligan! Wait up!"

On hearing his name Culligan turned, sat down his packets and waited.

Eddie's first words when they came face to face were ill-chosen. He said, "I bet I can tell you the name of your father." As soon as the words were out of his mouth Artie knew it was a mistake.

Culligan was still steady on his feet, and as a child he had known much ridicule and derisive speculation pertaining to the identity of his father. He was not in a happy frame of mind, and having the topic of his parenthood so smugly broached did not sit well. Culligan grabbed Artie up by his upper arms, walked him over to the edge of the dock and dropped Artie into the icy waters of the Hudson River.

• • •

Earl Bates said, "William Culligan then boarded the ferry headed up to Fort Lee and that is the last known location of this man Culligan." Rising from his desk and returning to the window, hands clasped behind his back, Earl Bates was lost in thought. Turning to face Serena, he said, "I would like you to locate this man. There is no longer any doubt that he is the son of Mary Culligan. I want you to determine if he knows the name of his father."

"Yes of course."

Earl Bates paused. His words barely audible, he said, "I need to make amends to Mary Culligan's son for the harm done to this fine young woman and to her son. I will require weekly dispatches, detailing your progress and expenses. Would that be acceptable?"

"This would be acceptable. Still, there is something more that has not been addressed. Why me? Why have you chosen me for this task?"

Earl Bates felt challenged to explain himself and continued to stare out the window into the wind-swept streets. Returning to his desk, he said, "The Pinkertons have demonstrated no ability to make contact with Culligan. All they have accomplished is identifying where he has been and nothing about where he is or where he is going."

"Is that the only reason I am being hired?"

"That, sadly, is not the only reason. The Pinkertons snuck up in the dark on Jesse James mother's window and threw in a bomb! The James boys were not even there but their mother was severely injured and a young boy was killed. That act demonstrated not only immorality but stupidity. No wonder they were unable to locate William Culligan." The anger in Earl Bates was then replaced by his usual glum demeanor.

"Is there something else?"

"You don't let up do you? I feel like I am being turned inside out! There is something else. I need someone to look into this man and report to me on the true content of his character. Colonel Kellogg has informed me you have a rare gift for detecting the true character of a man. That is why I sent for you."

Serena nodded and replied, "I understand."

"Do you now!" Earl Bates resumed a businesslike tone saying, "I take it you have found accommodations here in the city?"

"I have."

"Please return to this office tomorrow at 7 AM. At that time I will have a contract agreement drawn up. If you agree to the contract you will be provided with another advance on your salary and copies of all the information in my possession pertaining to this man Culligan."

Leaving the offices of Bates, Bates and Collier, Serena felt a sense of satisfaction. With completion of this assignment she might afford a property in or around London and maintain herself while establishing her career as a writer.

Chapter Six—Jeremiah is shot

As a spy Serena had asked few questions. Her usual technique began with her flawless assessment of the character of the parties involved.

It was during the early years of life within her family that Serena learned to never ask direct questions but listen for the oblique reference, what was *not* being said directly. It was precisely this mode of listening that allowed her to recognize that the issues Earl Bates Sr. wished addressed were not hers but his own family issues.

During the entire interview with Earl Bates, Serena had asked only two direct questions.

• • •

Serena arrived at the offices of Bates, Bates and Collier promptly at 7 AM. Contracts were ready for the signature of Serena McNabb and Earl Bates Sr. She reviewed the contract carefully and fully, and was pleased to find the contract generous. Her signature was witnessed by the company attorney.

Earl Bates then handed over copies of reports outlining all that he knew of a man who referred to himself simply as Culligan.

"It is my impression," Earl Bates said, "that this man Culligan would not drop a woman into icy waters." The parting remarks of Earl Bates were simple and direct. "I bid you good luck and God's speed."

• • •

Serena began inquiries on arrival in Fort Lee. She located a streetcar conductor who remembered a large man carrying a suitcase and gun case.

"Mostly," he confided, "The man was breathing fumes of bourbon and got off the streetcar at the railroad station."

Serena located a ticket seller who remembered a man fitting that description having bought a railroad ticket for Memphis, Tennessee. In Memphis, inquiry revealed that Culligan, now sober, had booked passage on a sternwheeler bound for New Orleans. Serena then booked passage for New Orleans.

• • •

Using the time afforded, Serena sorted through and read the reports detailing all that was known of this man Culligan. Some of the notes contained little more than dates and concrete references. These reports were reviewed and set aside. Other reports, however, provided Serena with a flavor of the man, and these reports she read and reread.

• • •

At the close of the Civil War, Ethan Joins, a man noted for his curiosity, had burrowed about in California, and talked to everyone. Following vague rumors led Ethan into the Oregon Territory and then on to Vancouver, BC. It was there he learned that a man named Culligan had made a gold strike upriver. Culligan never revealed the location of that strike, saying only that the claim was played out.

Ethan Joins tied his horse to the hitching post. Entering Jeremiah Doty's Trading Post, Ethan said, "You seem to carry a little bit of everything along with trading in skins."

"I do. Got lucky," Jeremiah said, "got me a decent wife and a decent store."

"I hear that William Culligan is a friend of yours."

Jeremiah paused . . . "You are not from this part of the country. Up here we knew him only by the name Culligan."

"I came up from California and there too, no one knew Culligan's first name, if he even had a first name."

"So how did you come to know Culligan's first name?"

"His father hired me to find the son he'd never met."

• • •

Jeremiah invited Ethan to have dinner with him and his wife. Jeremiah's wife, named Lonesome, was a large Indian woman known to chop wood with the best of them.

After dinner the two men set themselves in the flickering light in front of the open fireplace. After each man lit his pipe, Jeremiah exhaled a cloud of smoke and admitted, "I'm not all that proud of how I came to know Culligan."

"Jeremiah, anything you say will remain private and only for the ear of Culligan's father back in Boston."

The dam broke and the story gushed forth.

"You want me to tell you about Culligan. It was him shot and killed my brother Thomas. Hell! I might as well start back at the beginning. My brother got in some trouble back in Chicago. He couldn't hold any job for long because he expected other men to carry his load for him—plus him being a thief. After getting caught with his hand in the till, the Judge gave him the choice of either joining the Army or going to jail. Thomas jumped at the chance to join the Army. The war had just begun and my brother seemed to believe that the Army would be a grand and glorious adventure. He thought the Army would quickly recognize his true value. Unfortunately, they surely did recognize his true value.

"Since I was the oldest and mother was widowed, I could have avoided being taken by the Army. It was plain to see that Thomas was taller and better looking than me and was my mother's favorite.

"Thomas quickly recognized that the Army was not for him, and Mother, on her deathbed, got me to promise that I would take Thomas up into Canada, keep him out of the war, and out of jail."

"You took him into Canada?"

"I did. It was true enough that he probably would not have survived the War. His Company suffered the fate of most units during the War. Half his original Company died of pneumonia, typhoid, cholera, scurvy, and other diseases. Half of those who hadn't died of sickness died in battle."

"After taking Thomas up into Canada I bought a shotgun and we started working our way toward the west coast and as far away from the war as we could get.

"You found work along the way?"

"I found work in Winnipeg as a storekeeper, while Thomas did odd jobs. In the month of January in the Year of 1862 I met Suzy Slam. We made plans to marry in the Spring—then Thomas got drunk and grabbed ahold of the store owner's wife."

Ethan nodded, "And you ran for your lives."

"Damn sure did! Heading west we found work sometimes but it never lasted long and then we would move a little more westward. My brother stole a passed out drunk's Navy Colt, stuck it a bucket of lard, and buried it where he could dig it up after we finished with the haying.

"Still, for two Chicago boys being stuck out there on the open plains, we weren't doing too bad. This all changed when my brother made advances on a rancher's daughter.

"Again—we ran for our lives.

"We traveled west to a point where we were close up on the mountains and crossed a soggy meadow that had once been a beaver pond. The stream feeding the pond had washed down dirt that filled the pond, turned it into a soggy meadow, and swarms of mosquitoes were rising from still pools.

"Once we were off the meadow and on firmer ground, we happened on the tracks of a man wearing a heavy pair of boots. We figured those tracks had been made by a white man with good boots. The two of us were a sorry looking pair by this time. Our pack mule had died some time back, leaving us to carry what gear we had. There was only four days worth of flour and beans left. We were poorly equipped, our boots were about wore out, and our clothes were about to fall off. We lived on what little game I had been able to bag including porcupine."

Ethan Joins nodded. "I had porcupine once. Not good."

Jeremiah echoed, "Not good. I had my shotgun and my brother had the Colt revolver he stole. Neither of us had ever fired a gun before the Army. Considering our lack of wilderness experience and our inexperience with firearms, it was a miracle we made it that far.

"We grew up in the bustle of Chicago, and having gone to work as storekeepers at an early age, neither of us were prepared for the solitude of traveling across the plains. The quiet and the aloneness gave me the jitters. Then we came across another man's tracks, they were made by a large man either weighing about 300 pounds or he was carrying a heavy pack. Our luck had taken a turn for the better. And these tracks looking fresh, we figured he's not more than a day ahead of us."

Ethan said, "Was this Culligan?"

"Turned out it was. Thomas thought we should be able to catch up with him soon enough.

"Even though my brother hadn't said anything about robbing the man, I knew he was thinking on it. Out in this wilderness, with no chance of being found out, I thought my brother might backshoot any man having something he wanted."

"Was that true?"

"Turned out," Jeremiah said, "to be too-damn true."

Jeremiah's wife Lonesome was hovering about and looking concerned.

Sighing, Jeremiah announced, "I'm sort of tired. I'm going to finish my pipe and go to bed. If you like we can talk tomorrow evening."

The following evening the two men again set themselves up in front of the fireplace. In the flickering light Jeremiah tamped tobacco into his pipe, picked a burning ember out of the fireplace, lit his pipe, and settled back to continue his story.

"I told you about that meadow. We left that meadow quick enough. There were swarms of mosquitoes rising from the still pools that dotted the meadow. We figured the man we were following must be a prospector. The trail took us south until we reached a broad creek and then the trail led westward along the creek.

"I will say one thing. It was my brother who spotted a pool alongside the creek. A drop in the water level had trapped two trout. It wasn't that hard to fetch those trout. We judged, being storekeepers, that we each had two pounds of fresh trout. Full bellies revived our spirits and our steps."

"Feast or famine," Ethan said, "Always seems to go that way in the bush."

"Mostly famine for us. Come evening we made camp. We

thought we would have caught up with the man ahead of us, him carrying a heavy pack, but it didn't look to me like we had gained much ground. Thomas kept saying that he couldn't be that far ahead, but hopelessness had creeped into his voice.

"I had almost dropped off to sleep when my brother said that the man we were following had to be a prospector, and he must be carrying gold. My brother's spirits had lifted and he yammered all night about what he could do with the gold."

"Your brother," Ethan said, "seems to be up and down, flat one minute and excited the next."

Jeremiah nodded. "I thought that the prospector might let us know where he found the gold . . . that we might go back and get our own gold. I tried to talk to Thomas about doing our own prospecting, but the look he gave me, when I suggested we not rob the stranger, was a look I had never seen before. It left me plumb scared!"

"When we were back on trail I tried to caution Thomas it might not do much good to backshoot the man we were following since his backpack would stop any shots from getting through. I warned my brother that it might not be as easy to bring this man down as he thought. I might as well have been talking to the wind. Nothing was going to dampen my brother's mood."

"Thomas cackled: 'Then we just have to get him when he's stopped to camp or when he's taking a crap. I tell you brother, tomorrow we're going to be rich men!'"

"It sounds," Ethan said, "as if your brother had gone plumb crazy."

"Thinking back, it does. I drifted in and out of sleep. I don't know whether it was guilt or dread that troubled me the most. All night long I heard my brother yammering about what he was going to do with the gold. At dawn light, we broke camp and resumed our journey downstream. Tracking the man was not difficult since he was following along the path taken by this small excuse of a river. Then the ground grew rougher.

"The midday sun had taken the chill off our bones when we came across the remains of Culligan's morning campfire. The fire pit was still warm and we knew he could not be all that far ahead of us.

"As we began dropping down off the higher ground the travel grew more rugged. The waters we were following began to rush faster on its downward path.

"We had not caught up with Culligan when failing light forced us to make camp. The following morning we came down to a river, a river we had not known about. Then I saw a Sharps rifle leaning against a boulder and came across his pack. The pack was heavy enough that it was all I could do to lift it.

"Then I did the dumbest thing I ever did in my life; I turned away, let my brother get behind me . . . I heard the sound of my brother drawing down on the hammer."

Ethen nodded. "Your brother shot you."

"He did. When I came to I was laying on the ground and the sun was setting in the West. My head was bloody and a stranger was standing and staring down at me. I saw my brother lying on the ground and I said, "You shot my brother."

The stranger's mouth dropped open, then closed, and he said: "That back-shooting bastard was your *brother?* I was watching the two of you when he shot you. When I stepped out from where I was watching, your brother turned on seeing me, and I shot him dead."

Chapter Seven—On to Vancouver

Serena, standing at the sternwheeler's rail, pondered on where this man Culligan could be. She returned to her cabin and again took up Robert Jourdan's Report. It stated that banker Will Pennypeck had once worked a decent claim upstream from the boy Culligan's poorer claim. Jourdan had asked Will Pennypeck about the rumor that as a boy Culligan had shot and killed four men, Will Pennypeck responded with some irritation saying, "I know all about that! I was working my own claim up on the Rosebud at the time. Those were dangerous times and Jerry Lawless was a real mean man and not to be trusted. His sidekick was kind of feeble-minded. Everyone called him Minnow. He followed Jerry Lawless around like a love-sick puppy, doing whatever Jerry Lawless said. Sometimes Lawless was seen to pat Minnow on his butt and Minnow would giggle in appreciation. On that day Lawless and Minnow were walking on the path alongside Rosebud Creek. My own claim was worth the working and upstream from Culligan's sorry claim.

"There was no law in the territory, and people got nervous when Jerry Lawless was about. He was mean and he was dangerous. Lawless stopped, gave Culligan a look, and then moved on. Culligan had been facing Lawless, saw the look, but kept on shoveling sand and gravel into his sluicebox.

"Lawless then had second thoughts . . . .. Shortly he was back with Minnow in tow. The boy Culligan carried a Colt in 36 caliber where it rode comfortable and unseen under the pullover shirt that dropped down past his waistband.

"Lawless returned with that big dragoon pistol in his hand. For all intents, Culligan was already dead. Lawless said, 'Boy! I'll give you just ten seconds to get'—Minnow giggled—and at the same time Culligan's thumb raised up that pull-down shirt, pulled his Colt and put two shots into Jerry Lawless.

"Lawless was dead before he finished talking. It took a moment for Minnow to realize what happened, but when he did, howling in rage, he went for Lawless's dragoon pistol and Culligan had to shoot that poor fool as well. Nobody could blame Culligan for what he had to do.

"It all happened so fast I don't think Culligan had time to think about what he was doing— he just did it! I can tell you we all slept easier with Jerry Lawless gone."

Robert Jourdan said, "That would have made Culligan a hero?"

"He was beardless, only 17 years old, but he was more level-headed than most of the men I knew, and he was not a hero to himself . . . but he did lay claim to the Dragoon pistol Lawless had carried. The general consensus was that claim jumpers needed hanging, so Jerry Lawless and Minnow were hung up as a warning to others."

"Did it work?"

"It did not. Murietta and his gang staged a raid on our camp. Again, it was Culligan got off the first shots and with that big Dragoon pistol. In only twenty days Culligan had shot and killed four men. For an otherwise quiet and beardless youth he sure had a knack for killing.

"Culligan broke camp two days later, left his sluice box and sold his shovel. He flat-out disappeared. I never saw him again until the day he came off that stagecoach from San Francisco and made a deposit in my bank. Culligan remembered me and trusted me from the time he was a boy."

"You have any idea where he might have been going?"

Will Pennypeck shook his head. "No idea. I'm not sure even Culligan knew where he was headed."

• • •

An additional report stated that on returning to San Francisco, Robert Jourdan chanced to come across hooker Rosie Conyers.

Rosie said, "Big Frenchy insisted I was his woman—that I worked for him. I left, but he followed and found me in the bar I was working. To teach me a lesson he ripped off my blouse leaving my upper body exposed. Culligan was sitting at a back table reading a book. He put down his book, took his coat off the back of the chair and draped it over my shoulders. He had a pistol holstered in his waistband and his shirt flopped down over it. Big Frenchy went for his gun but Culligan was quicker and left Big Frenchy stretched out dead on the barroom floor. Culligan went back to his table, picked up his book, and then he was gone."

"You ever see him again?"

"I never did. If you find him, tell him I still keep his coat for him."

Reading this, Serena thought, *So. Culligan is both a gunfighter and a gentleman.* She took another walk around the chilly deck before returning to the report by Ethan Joins.

• • •

Jeremiah had said, "Culligan had placed me on my bedroll and left a canteen of water close at hand. I was still dizzy and weak and the littlest movement wore me out. I rolled to the edge of my bedroll and pissed on the ground. Then I rolled back on my bedroll and struggled with the canteen for a drink of water. God was I thirsty. The ground started to spin and I passed out. When I came to the sun was high. Sometimes I could hear the sound of the stranger's ax. I woke up next morning and saw Culligan squatting on his haunches not ten feet away and watching me. He cleared his throat and said, 'My name's Culligan. You've been out the better part of a day and night. It looks like you may not be ready to die. I shaped the outside of my canoe this time last year. The salmon began their run so I smoked me some salmon before returning to my claim. The salmon will be starting their run soon and then I can smoke us some salmon. Meanwhile I can finish hollowing out our canoe."

Our canoe?

"If you live I'll be taking the two of us down the Frazier River to Vancouver. It will be some crowded, but not too much." Culligan turned to leave. After taking about five steps he stopped and said, "I haven't talked to another soul for three long years, so I won't be minding the company."

"Even though Culligan had not talked to anyone in three years, he still had a strong, rich voice and wrapped his tongue around hard words with ease."

"That evening, as dark was settling in, Culligan admitted, 'I don't much need the company of other men. Mostly I keep to myself. But all alone the last three years, I hungered to hear another voice. So nighttimes, and especially on those winter months when I was snowed in, I recited the play Hamlet from beginning to end. The words of Shakespeare spoke to me through my own voice."

Jeremiah had days of listening to the sound of Culligan's ax working on that canoe. Culligan used fire and ax to hollow out the inside of the canoe. "I tell you, when he finished that canoe it was a thing of beauty. Then he walked into the woods with my brother's empty pack. He came back with a full pack.

"Gold," Culligan said, "had eluded me often enough that I wasn't going to leave any behind. Out of plain cussedness I worked my claim until it was played out."

"The salmon run was plentiful. Culligan and me, we ate as much of the fresh salmon as we could choke down in preparation for the trip down river. Culligan smoked the rest. When he had what he judged was enough of the smoked salmon, he worked the canoe down to the river.

"Like I said, that canoe was a thing of beauty! I was still weak and not much use. Culligan made me comfortable in the bow and I watched as he loaded the canoe with supplies and what I judged must be close up to 200 pounds of gold dust and nuggets. With me in the bow and Culligan in the stern he pushed off for the trip down river. Going down river we talked some but not much. Culligan's eyes were always on the river or the land we were going through. He listened to everything I said but his eyes were always on the river and the land. I guess I did most of the talking. My brother was lying with the fishes and it shames me to admit I was feeling relief from the weight of responsibility for my brother's keeping."

"How come he didn't shoot you and leave you behind?"

Jeremiah nodded. "One time I asked him about that. He didn't answer right away. He said, 'I have known some sad times, especially when my mother died, when I did not much give a damn whether I lived or died, and only stubbornness kept me going. It was seeing the sadness in your eye, you being shot by your own brother, rather than seeing meanness mirrored in your eye. I think seeing the sad was what stayed my hand.'

"Culligan was mostly silent when we were on the river. But in bits and pieces I learned he came from New York City. As a boy he sold newspapers on the street and sold the fish he caught at the Fulton Fish Market. Mostly he fished for sturgeon. His mother died when he was real young. After her funeral he took up the money saved, fitted himself up with a backpack, a bedroll, and took the ferry over to New Jersey. He started walking in a westward direction. Along the way he bought a Hawkin rifle. Already having experience fishing, in time he learned something about hunting as well. When he found work, he worked. When he didn't have work he hunted, fished, and mostly lived off the land. Once he got lucky and got himself a bear. Not ever having skinned a bear before and then getting the hide cured was about the hardest and most frustrating task he ever took on, but he said that bearskin had come in real handy come winter."

"Culligan told me that his first winter alone was real hard. Buying the Hawkin rifle had used up a big chunk of the money his mother and he had saved. In bad weather he built lean-to's or hunkered down in whatever shelter he could find. When the weather cleared he would snowshoe on. The snow was deep that first winter and that was bad for the deer but good for Culligan. Snowshoeing on, twice he came across deer that had been confined to a small area by deep snow, built temporary shelters, and rested up until deer meat ran low.

"His first year alone was hard, but second year he bullcooked from early April to the middle of September for a crew laying railroad track. Bullcooking was keeping the kitchen and the crew's living cars stocked with firewood and water.

"Someone threw away a pair of worn-out boots and Culligan took the still-good leather from the top of the boots and worked on them each night as he built holsters to house his Colts.

"During the almost-six months he bullcooked for that railroad gang, Culligan had not spent one penny of his wages. When the track crew closed down he headed west while doing what chores he could find and sometimes selling the fish he caught or the deer he shot. Mostly he was saving his money and living off the land and it was a hard living and with no frills."

Culligan had headed for the Oregon Trail.

• • •

One evening, after bringing the canoe ashore and setting up camp, Culligan said, "In the time after my mother died I had walked over a thousand miles and was as good a shot with the Colt and Hawkin long gun as any man. I was dressed in a buckskin shirt, buckskin leggings, wearing moccasins, and had bought a wide-brimmed hat. My hair was hanging down my back and tied at the back of my neck. I was real young, but big for my age and even without a beard, I looked like a real mountain man.

"Out on the field outside Independence, men were testing their skill with firearms. I joined them and my skill with firearms was noted.

"I had thought about joining up with a horseback party heading to Oregon but by the time I got to Independence I was hearing reports of men traveling by horseback having their horses stolen by Indians or otherwise having lost their horses. Those traveling by wagon train did not ride. They walked along the side of their wagons and ate the dust or mud stirred up by the mules or oxen.

• • •

When Jeremiah and Culligan arrived in Vancouver BC, Culligan cashed in his gold at the bank and gave a buckskin poke of nuggets to Jeremiah.

"More than anything," Culligan said, "I am looking forward to a bath, haircut and beard trim." Culligan took himself to the best haberdashery in Vancouver and purchased all new linen from the skin out, pants, shirt, vest, coat, hat, and the best walking boots money could buy. After a long, luxurious bath he left his old clothes behind. Then, after a haircut, beard-trim, and boot-shine, he took himself to the best restaurant in town for a beefsteak, baked potato, string beans, and a wedge of apple pie. He followed the meal with a cigar and a glass of bourbon. Now sleepy yet hungering for something to read, he purchased a copy of Shakespeare's play *Macbeth*.

• • •

Chapter Eight—Banker Will Pennypeck

That first night in Vancouver, Culligan lolled about in the luxury of his hotel room, rested some, took another bath, read some more, and slept.

Culligan always awoke at first light. He returned to his room after an early breakfast and stretched out on the bed with his copy of Shakespeare's *Macbeth*.

There was a knock on the door and the sound of Lulu Collins voice saying, "Room service."

Culligan took up the Colt, unlocked the door, checked the hallway to see if anyone was lurking. The hallway was clear—so he let in the chambermaid and her cart, closed the door, locked it, and only then did he allow himself to smile and say, "Yours is the first woman's voice I heard in three years." That wasn't quite true, he had heard other female voices the day before, but it was close enough.

Chambermaid Lulu Collins was fulsome, older than Culligan, but not too much, and had dark brown hair. First, she surveyed the bathroom and then said, "So you struck it rich. You are a good looking man Mister Culligan. Are you also a generous man Mister Culligan?"

"I am."

"Then I suppose I can be generous too." She pulled her dress up over her head and said, "Get undressed. I don't have much time."

The next morning Lulu arrived early. Afterwards, with the two of them cupped together like two spoons, Culligan said, "You have children."

"Two of them. How did you know?"

"Stretch marks."

"Ah. Marcus is eleven and Benjy is nine. I am not able to have more children."

They kissed.

"My husband was a good man and a good father. He got killed in a logging accident."

"I sort of wondered about that. Raising two children after losing a husband, that's hard."

"I will do whatever is needed to protect my children."

Culligan climbed out of the bed and began to pace. Lulu rolled over on her side, raised up on her elbow, and watched. With downcast eyes, Culligan circled the room.

Lulu had a puzzled look on her face and said, "What?"

"My mother was like you. She was alone and did whatever was needed to take care of me."

Culligan and Lulu were more like friends than lovers. Still, they laughed, kissed, and then kissed again.

• • •

Calmed after four days of Lulu's ministrations, well-rested and with his hide, hair, and beard now scrubbed clean of all traces of smoke and grime, Culligan visited the gunsmith. "What I want from you is another hideaway gun. I want it in 44 Remington with the barrel cut to three inches and a dovetail sight on the barrel and with a spare cylinder."

The gunsmith said, "Pay in advance. First order I've had for what is called the Avenging Angel."

"You have anyone around here good at making custom-built holsters?"

"Norse Leather Works is one block down and on the other side of the street."

• • •

When Culligan received the Remington Avenging Angel and the extra cylinder, he took them for a walk out of town. The workings and the accuracy of the Avenging Angel proved satisfactory. He walked back, and when he opened the door to Norse Leatherworks, a tinkling bell announced his presence. Sven Tollefson came in from the back of his shop. Culligan laid the Avenging Angel on the counter and said, "You think you could design me a holster that would fit in my waistband?"

Sven adjusted his glasses and muttered, "Right or left handed?"

"Right handed."

"You staying at the Grand?"

"I am."

"Come back tomorrow morning and I'll have it for you."

Culligan nodded. "That's quick enough."

• • •

The holster was satisfactory. As a belly gun the Remington rode to the left of his belt-buckle and comfortable in Culligan's waistband. Culligan then went looking for Jeremiah Doty. Having traveled down river with him he had grown to appreciate his company. Jeremiah was still in town. Having already turned over to him a buckskin poke of nuggets, Culligan now left him his 36 caliber Colt, the Dragoon pistol, and all his old possessions including the Sharps rifle and the canoe.

Jeremiah would be setting up his own trading post up-river.

• • •

On a bright early morning, their last morning together, Culligan presented Lulu with an additional chunk of money. Lulu looked at the money, looked at Culligan and said, "I asked you, that first time, if you were a generous man. You are indeed, Mister Culligan, you are indeed. This will allow me to open up the finest boarding house in Vancouver."

Culligan went to the bank, closed out much of his account and left with a Gladstone bag holding a change of clothes and a sizeable chunk of money. Plus, he had cash and gold certificates in a waterproof money belt when he boarded the ship Ida May, which then set sail for San Francisco on the outgoing tide.

• • •

Serena McNabb read and reread the report by Ethan Joins. She could not escape the impression that Culligan was an isolate who preferred the works of William Shakespeare to the company of other men. Serena concluded that he would be inclined to grow restless and keep moving rather than settle in one place. Other reports did not dispute this impression.

Yet, she thought, *he did reach out to Jeremiah Doty and Lulu Collins.*

• • •

Robert Jourdan's report stated that Culligan landed in San Francisco and took a stagecoach to Sacramento where Will Pennypeck had his bank.

Will was a dignified and small-boned man with glasses and stood almost 6 feet tall and weighed almost 160 pounds. Formally dressed in a three-piece suit, underneath his coat, he carried a derringer in his vest pocket. After scratching out a decent profit in gold out of the Rosebud, Will Pennypeck had begun—in small ways—providing banking services.

One thing everyone knew was that Will Pennypeck could be trusted. Therefore, when others made strikes, as Culligan was doing now, they traveled to Will Pennypeck for banking services.

Culligan said, "When I heard you had your own bank, I figured you would have put on a round belly like a good banker should, but you still have the lean look you had when we were up on the Rosebud . . . you haven't changed that much."

Will saw a large muscular and vigorous man dressed in a gray-blue suit and a tan vest. "If you had not told me, I never would have recognized you as the boy living the life of a grown man up on the Rosebud. Now you look at least 50 pounds heavier plus you have a short full beard. I heard you made a good strike up north and then disappeared."

"Will, I need the services of a banker I can trust and I always did trust you."

Serena learned that the two men had sat in front of Will's open fireplace, sipping bourbon and talking over old times up on the Rosebud. The next day, after concluding their banking business, Culligan left Sacramento.

Chapter Nine—The Oregon Trail

Culligan had some experience on horseback, while Cassy and Larco had none at all. But with every passing day they grew more accustomed to life in the saddle. In those times when they walked their horses, it came clear that Culligan was more comfortable being on foot—definitely he was a walker— while Cassy and Larco preferred being on horseback.

Larco observed Culligan's practice of firing one live round with the Spencer and then dry-firing the spent cartridge three more times before ejecting the fired round and chambering in a live round. Seeing this, Larco adopted the same practice. He was surprised to discover that dry-firing helped improve his accuracy as much as if he were firing only live ammunition. Larco was encouraged to continue practicing with the Winchester—and he was getting better every day. Culligan, when he practiced, would stuff cotton in his ears and tie a bandanna around his head to preserve his hearing. Larco didn't bother.

• • •

What with having enough to eat, Cassy began to fill out and the skinny young girl, who Culligan had assumed would always remain thin, was being transformed. Her hips and shoulders spread, she was growing a bust, and her arms, legs, and her butt grew more fulsome.

The skinny girl was turning into an attractive young woman. Noting this, Culligan purchased the five-shot Pocket Model Colt in 32 cap and ball, holstered it, and handed it over to Cassy. She spent the rest of the day focused on the Colt. Even in her bedroll she would hold it up and stare at it by the flickering light of the campfire. The next afternoon Culligan handed Cassy a knapsack that contained all that was needed for the maintenance of the Colt.

Cassy practiced shooting, reloading, and shooting again, until the works became fouled. She was instructed to take the Colt apart, clean and oil, and then put it back together. It took her until almost-dark. After she had completed the re-assembly, Culligan walked by and said, "Good! At first it takes a long time. After you've done it a few more times you will clean and assemble again in minutes. My first handgun was a Colt and the first time it took me almost all day to clean and put it back together. Now, even with my eyes closed, I can take the Remington apart, clean all the parts, and put them back together, oil everything, reload, and I am good to go."

Culligan said, "Cassy, when the time comes, don't think about it, just do it. I've killed nine men, counting the Affleck Brothers, and each of them was intent on killing me. If you hesitate, take time to ask yourself what to do, unless the other fellow is even more slow-witted than you, you are already dead."

• • •

The weather was mellow. They traveled while not being hard on the horses or on themselves. Their horsemanship continued to improve while they took great care of their mounts. They grew comfortable living in the open and comfortable with each other.

They were not, however, all that comfortable with being in Georgia.

Sherman's burning of Atlanta plus the scorched earth policy as his troops savaged the land in their march to the sea, while it guaranteed Lincoln's re-election in the North, it left Yankee's downright unpopular in Georgia. Anyone riding with a colored was definitely a Yankee. They did not rush, but they did not linger as they passed through Georgia.

On a clear moonlit night in Alabama, while lying in their bedrolls, they heard a wolf baying at the moon. Culligan sat up and howled back, the wolf answered, and then Culligan answered the wolf. The sound Culligan made was so real that it gave Larco the shivers.

Larco said, "Cully, you travel all the way to Oregon with those fellows you started out with?"

Culligan paused . . . "Sixteen days out we were coming up on Fort Kearney. Knute Hanson had the predawn watch, the most dangerous time. He was sleeping when he was supposed to be standing watch. So we left him sleeping and moved on. There were seven of us in our party when we reached Fort Kearney. Then Able and Samuel came down sick with cholera. Two days later both of them were dead.

"Cholera was always a part of the Trail but the bad cholera years were 1849, 1850, and 1852. Those were the epidemic years for cholera on the Oregon Trail. Not wanting to catch cholera from the others, when I left Fort Kearney, I left alone."

• • •

Once, having passed through Alabama and into Mississippi, they came up on a sparkling little stream. Culligan said, "You see that branch in there stripped of bark and with the ends gnawed off? There's beaver upstream and they have fouled the water."

They rode upstream until they were a mile above the beaver pond. Culligan said, "You drink water downstream from a beaver pond or where a dead animal is in the water and you could get serious sick and maybe die. I saw plenty of that on the Platte River.

"I walked over 2,000 miles in four months. There were those at outposts along the way that would count the number coming through. Greatest migration of all time. Even greater than when Moses took his people out of Egypt. The Mormon migration along the trail began in 1846 and there were less than 3,000 on the Trail that year.

"I jumped on the Trail in April of 1847 and that year there were 7,000 of us on the Trail.

"You being well armed," Larco said, "and able to handle yourself, I expect others would welcome traveling with you."

"They did. There was a group of eight fellows having set up camp for the night. I laid out my bedroll a 100 yards down from them and in case of rain I set up my small tent. They were watching me while not being obvious about it. I picked up a piece of dried-out horseshit and tossed it up in the air while drawing one of my Colts and I blew that horseshit all apart. Usually I pull off that trick in about one of four or five tries but, having pulled it off first try I decided to stop while I was ahead.

"The trick to that shot is firing at exactly the moment when that piece of horseshit has reached as high as it will go and starts to drop."

The next morning Culligan was chewing on smoked venison and waiting for his cup with coffee to cool down when George Gannett, having his own cup of coffee in hand, walked down to young Culligan's campsite.

"Morning," he said.

"Morning."

"The eight of us are on foot, same as you. We got us one mule and that two wheeled wagon to carry tent and supplies and we expect to walk twenty miles each day til we get to Fort Leavenworth. You traveling that way?"

"I am."

"You think you could keep up that pace?"

"I been known to cover thirty miles in a day, what with carrying a heavy pack."

By the time the party reached Fort Leavenworth Culligan had checked out the party and the party had checked out Culligan. He was invited to join them on the Oregon Trail.

Culligan accepted.

"Larco, we left Fort Leavenworth and on that first day out, ahead of us, we could see men on horses strung out over about a mile and on the horizon we could see wagons creeping along. When we caught up with that party of twelve wagons, we saw them quarreling with the leader so we moved on. We did not take our own nooner til we were a good four miles ahead of them. Some of those wagon trains had a fog of discontent so thick you could cut it with a knife."

Larco raised the question, "Cully, how well did you and your party get along?"

"George Gannett was the leader and brooked no nonsense. There was a full moon the night Knute Hanson relieved me on my

Watch. He had the pre-dawn Watch. I had not been asleep long when Gannett woke me and the others up. We moved out quiet and by moonlight. Knute's friend Abel asked, "What about Knute?"

The Captain said, "Last I saw he had taken his bedroll into the brush and was sleeping sound when he was supposed to be on watch and making sure that some Indian did not get the chance to sneak in, cut our throats, and steal our mule. I thought about shooting him, but decided to let him keep on sleeping."

Grudgingly, Abel saw the wisdom of the Captain taking this action. "For myself," Culligan said, "I took pride in carrying my own weight."

"No horses," Larco said, "That must have been a hardship, having to walk twenty miles every day."

"For some, not for me."

"What about the covered wagons?"

"They had it the worst. Between April and May, when our party jumped on the Oregon Trail, there were already more than 5,000 immigrants on the Trail ahead of us.

"Those with the covered wagons had to walk same as us while having to find graze for the oxen that pulled their wagons, graze for their herds of cattle, and their horses. There were so many on the trail that those at the back of the pack found little graze for their livestock and sometimes had to leave the trail and travel some distance to find good graze.

"All this took time. Then they had to push their livestock even harder to make up for the time lost.

"Those that left too soon, what with stormy weather, their wagons would get bogged down in the mud and they and their stock were already worn out even before they got started. Rivers and streams became swollen and impassable and while they waited for the waters to lower they still had to find graze for their livestock.

"Along the trail and in the rivers and creeks were the dead bodies of horses, oxen, and cattle— they fouled the water and made it undrinkable— I saw stoves, the shattered wrecks of claw-footed tables, massive bureaus, other pieces of fine furniture, and even food sometimes dumped out of wagons to lighten the load."

• • •

One morning Larco startled a deer. It ran off before he could get off a shot. Larco and Cassy wanted to go after it and track it down. Culligan said, "Wait! You startle a deer, but not too much, it will run off and most times will circle back to get a look at what startled them. You need to figure out where they might be coming back and wait."

Larco got the deer with a headshot.

Each day, Larco and Cassy learned more, occasionally bagging a deer and once Larco bagged a wild pig. Culligan taught them how to dress out game and how to skin and tan hides while he made himself a pair of buckskin moccasins and a buckskin vest. Larco and Cassy watched and learned while Culligan built temporary smokehouses and showed them how to smoke venison and fish.

• • •

Culligan was used to living alone, keeping his thoughts to himself, and there were days when he hardly spoke a word.

Larco, on the other hand, had spent a lifetime living in close quarters with other men. He was a sociable and friendly fellow at home with story telling and jokes and being easy to like. He looked to be a peaceful and easygoing man and not a danger.

Looks can be deceiving.

Outside Butler, Alabama, they rented a small house and horse shed for the winter. They hunted, fished, rode some, and generally kept to themselves. On one of their town visits, when Larco went into the bar for a drink, one of the townspeople, a large man, having seen Larco ride up with Cassy, chose to make some disparaging remarks about any white man that would ride with a nigger. Larco heard. The townsman, alarmed at seeing Larco heading in his direction, turned his open palms upward saying, "I'm unarmed!"

Larco did not touch the Derringer riding in his vest and the larger and younger man threw a looping punch Larco avoided and then punching the townsman in the throat. The townsman was gagging and had both hands on his throat when Larco kicked his left leg out from under him and watched him thud down on the barroom floor.

Larco was squatting close to the man when he said, "I'm a peaceable sort of a man, but if you push this, you will end up dead! You think about that before you open your mouth again!"

The townsman was faced with the sobering realization that although Larco was the older and smaller man, he was also the better man.

Culligan had entered in time to see this. He was not a man to speak his approval of the way Larco handled things, but said, "Let's have a drink before moving on."

The bartender, a wise man, did not intrude in other people's business, and without a word he poured each of the men a drink. They tossed down their drinks, paid for them, left the bar, and rode out of town.

• • •

Cassy was quiet as they rode out. After a time she said, "That was about me wasn't it? You could have killed a man because of me!"

Culligan grunted, "Mind you girl, neither of us would be killing a man unless that man needed killing." Further on Culligan said, "That bigmouth you took down will have friends in the area."

It was decided this would be a good time to be moving on. The three friends moved on to Mississippi for the rest of the winter.

• • •

There came another night, while they were in Mississippi, when they heard a wolf howling at the moon. Culligan rose up out of his bedroll and replied with his own mournful howl. The wolf howled again and Culligan answered.

Larco said, "Second time I heard you howling back at a wolf. Your howling sounds as real as the wolf's. Where did you learn to make that howl?"

"There were eight or nine different trails starting from the Missouri river to where they all came together at Fort Kearny as the Oregon Trail. From there on we saw dead livestock along the trail and in the North Platte River. With all those immigrants firing away there was not much left in the way of game but there were dead livestock and there were wolves.

"I don't know why, but nighttime, when I heard them howling

at the moon, it brought me feelings of loneliness. When I howled back some of the lonely would go away."

"From that," Larco said, "there are some who might say you are more wolf than man."

Culligan Shrugged, "Maybe so."

• • •

Wind and rain greeted their arrival in Meridian, Mississippi. Miles out of town they rented a house for the winter.

Larco had a good singing voice and good pitch and entertained Cassy by singing the sea chanteys he had acquired from a lifetime at sea. It was an easy time and a reprieve from the hard life each of them had known. It was Larco who spent time relating to Cassy. He was her big brother. She liked him a lot yet it was always Culligan who turned the head of Cassy. Larco took no offense.

To himself Culligan admitted, *no one needs to know. For myself, I find Cassy a delight and the one I like more than any other young woman I ever met.*

He gave Larco and Cassy money each month. Once, stopping for supplies in a poor town, Cassy began showing off that she had money. Culligan was troubled by her doing something that stupid. Riding away from town, both Cassy and Larco could see that Culligan was stiller than usual. Two miles out of town Culligan still hadn't spoken. He dismounted, cut a strong switch, trimmed it, pulled Cassy from her horse and threw her to the ground. He gave her four good whacks while telling her, "Don't you ever show off you having money! You are a young black woman with good boots, well-mounted, and well-armed! In this poor land this is mean and will make trouble. Dammit! I already killed nine men! We have enough to worry about without you stirring up more trouble!"

Larco comforted Cassy, telling her that Culligan had been worried for her safety.

Cassy apologized and never again rubbed white folks noses in the fact that she had money while they had none.

• • •

Larco talked to Cassy all the time, entertained her with jokes and stories of the sea. Culligan watched and could not help but approve of the way Larco related to Cassy. For her part, Cassy felt secure and safe in the company of the men, and she forgave Culligan for the licking he gave her.

Chapter Ten—Meet Paul Thrum

At the close of the Civil War John Wesley Hardin was a fifteen year old Texas boy who shot and killed an unarmed black man for having done him some small slight. *Hardin was not arrested.* Later, he shot a man for snoring. He would one day own up to having killed 28 men. The Texas Rangers, however, claimed that he had killed more than forty.

• • •

Ryegate sat on the Northeast corner of two trails that crossed in East Texas. The town consisted of a livery stable, general store, a hotel, and a two-story combination saloon and whore-house painted bright red.

The horses and pack mule were about played out. So, afternoon, they set up camp west of Ryegate, watered the horses and mule, put them up in the Ryegate stable, hayed, grained, and rubbed them down. "Larco," Culligan said, "you stay with Cassy. I need to check things out."

Ryegate felt different with John Wesley Hardin in town. Only nineteen years old, Hardin was already a well-known gunfighter.

Culligan was on his second drink when Hardin approached. "Would you care for a game of chance?"

"Not today, Some other time."

"Your name Culligan?"

"It is."

"I hear you killed four men when you were seventeen?"

"So they say."

"You rely on the Avenging Angel. How accurate is it?"

"Some Avenging Angels have barrels less than three inches. Mine has three inches. It's accurate enough."

Hardin said, "Seems like the man with a short pecker would be the one to favor a short-barreled gun."

"Not that way at all. It's the man with a short pecker who needs the long-barreled gun."

"John," a friend called, "We need to start the game."

John Wesley Hardin said, "The game is calling me. But, we will meet again."

• • •

Next day, after breakfast, Culligan tucked in his shirt, leaving the Avenging Angel more accessible, and carried the Spenser in the crook of his left arm.

Watching, Larco and Cassy said nothing.

"You two—not much chance of my not coming back—but if you don't see me coming back there's money in my bedroll. Then the two of you go get the horses and light on out of here."

Larco picked up a pebble and threw it at a mesquite bush. "How much of a chance is that Cully?"

"Not much."

Hardin was sitting in front of the saloon and that was 60 yards past the stable. He saw that Culligan was carrying a long gun. Hardin got out of his chair and walked back into the saloon.

Culligan, grained and watered the horses and mule, then returned to camp.

The next morning Culligan returned to Ryegate for their livestock. When Cassy saw Cully ride back leading the other two horses and the pack-mule, she ran to meet him.

Larco said, "We heard no shots."

"Hardin pulled out last night. Hardin likes killing and he likes having people scared of him. My not being afraid and my not showing my back, I think that told him something."

• • •

On the edge of San Antonio, Paul Thrum, a tall black man about Larco's age, with a spattering of grey in his hair and beard, wearing spectacles, was standing in front of the saloon as Culligan, Cassy, and Larco were riding up.

Seeing Paul Thrum drop his hand on the Navy Colt sitting butt forward on his right hip, Culligan said, "Cassy, you hold up now." Larco branched off twenty feet to the left while Culligan rode off twenty feet to the right. Cassy had pulled up twenty feet in front of Paul Thrum. She said, "What?"

In Gulla, a language neither Larco or Culligan could understand, Paul asked, "Are those white men using you?"

"No! These are my friends." Turning, she said, "Cully, Larco, you stand down. He only wants to protect me."

Those two white men are her friends? Could this be? It took time for this to sink into Paul Thrum's brain. Slowly, his hand retreated from the Navy Colt.

Larco then saddle booted the Winchester. Quietly, he said, "You being out to protect Cassy, let me buy you a drink."

Larco and Paul entered and bellied up to the bar. A black man and a white man drinking together raised the hackles of some. Then seeing Culligan enter and joining them, hackles smoothed back down. Seeing Culligan had that effect on people.

• • •

Paul was invited to ride with them. Well past San Antonio, they set up camp. Then Paul and Cassy went for a walk. Cassy said, "Paul, what was it like for you?"

"Hard. Real hard. I was much troubled seeing young black girls being used by white men."

"Paul," Cassy said, "Larco, Culligan, and me, we slept side by side many a night. Neither man ever touched me that way. I hope you will be my friend too."

Head slowly moving side to side, Paul said, "This is a lot to take in. I was one of twenty slaves on the plantation where I was born.

79

When the Union Army came near, all but me ran to the Union Army thinking they would free them, while I was running in the opposite direction. The Union Army gathering up the friends I had known my whole life and returning them to their Master. I ran from Tennessee damn near all the way to Chicago.

"I was in the Union Army's first black troop and I took whatever I could from white southerners. By the end of the war I had me a Navy Colt, a horse, a Spenser carbine, some hard cash, and I bought me some spectacles."

• • •

Larco cautioned that Culligan might be getting ready to leave them. Cassy shook her head—did not want to think that.

There came a time when Larco was working with Cassy on numbers and Culligan called out to her. She turned to look and Culligan lobbed a rock at her head. She ducked away from the rock. She peered at Culligan with a questioning look that said, Why?

"Good." Culligan said, "You ducked first and asked why later. That's what you do in a gunfight. Cassy, you carry a gun and the day will come when a white man will take it in his head to shoot your black ass. If you stop to think about whether to shoot a white man, or any man, you are already dead. Don't think about it. Shoot the son-of-a- bitch and keep on shooting until he goes down! You can think about it later . . . you can even feel bad about it if you want to, but do it later."

The next morning, after rolling out of their bedrolls and having breakfast, Culligan said, "When that ship sunk out from under me and Larco, I had been headed for New York to visit my mother's grave. I need to do that. Then come warm weather I'll be heading back to look up the three of you. I only know two ways of living. One of them is logging and that is a dangerous life and good only for a young man and not for a woman.

"Also, I know about prospecting. That is a hard life mostly with the loneliness of it and the disappointment of working claims that pay little or no more than a day's wage. Men have been known to go mad what with the loneliness and disappointment of it.

Still, when I get back, and if the three of you want to learn about prospecting, I'll teach you what I know about that life, which is considerable. I'm leaving the pack-mule with the three of you."

They remained silent while Culligan saddled his horse and tied his bedroll and saddlebags behind the saddle. "I'll be back and look you up in the Spring."

Larco said, "Where you headed now Cully?"

Culligan mounted up before answering. "I'll be heading back to San Antonio, sell my horse, and take the stage to New Orleans. I want to catch a steamboat going up the Mississippi. That is one fine river and I want to see more of it." Looking down at the three of them he said, "You three get along well enough and you need to be partnered up when I get back."

Culligan then rode off a distance, stopped, looked back, and waved to them. They waved back and watched as he rode away.

Cassy said, "Larco, will we ever see him again?" Musing on this Larco said, "I don't know Cassy—I just don't know." Then Larco assured her, "Don't you worry little sister. Me and Paul, we're going to stick with you and we'll do fine."

• • •

Larco, Paul and Cassy wintered in Cuidad, Mexico. Larco said, "Even in winter this place is hot. I'd sure hate being here mid-summer."

Springtime, they rode back into Texas. Cowboys looking for work often showed up on foot, unarmed, and not even having their own saddle. A middle-age seaman, a middle-aged black man, and a young black girl, were not the usual hands Swartzkoff was looking for but these three were well armed, well-mounted, and willing to work for poor pay.

"Paul," Larco said, "have you ever smiled in your life?"

"Never saw anything to smile about."

• • •

Paul was puzzled. He watched and listened. Larco was patient with Cassy, he saw that she was fond of Larco, but she always wanted to talk about Culligan. "Larco," Paul said, "Why did you and Culligan take on the caring for Cassy?"

"She brought us water."

Paul nodded. "She seems to think Culligan will be coming back."

"He said he will. He's a hard man to kill and if he lives, he'll be back."

• • •

Culligan completed his business in New York. Then, first by train and then by Mississippi sternwheeler, he returned to New Orleans. A newspaper report informed Culligan that the distinguished Shakespearian actor Kerry Blackstone and his acting troop were now putting on a production of the play Hamlet. Culligan had a great love for the works of William Shakespeare and reserved a front row seat for a ten day run of the play.

He was having a drink in the hotel bar where the actors congregated after their performance and standing next to the actress who played Gertrude. She looked on Culligan with speculation in her eyes, said, "I think you are the same man I see sitting in that front row seat for three nights running."

Culligan admitted it was him. "This is my first chance to see the play even though I know every line of the play by heart."

In a disbelieving and falsetto voice Gertrude responded, "Oh Really!" Then she provided Culligan with his cue:

GERTRUDE: "Thou know'st 'tis common: all that lives must die,

Passing through nature to eternity."

CULLIGAN: "Ay, madam, it is common."

GERTRUDE: "If it be, why seems it so particular with thee?"

CULLIGAN : "Seems, madam! Nay, it is: I know not 'seems.'

'Tis not alone my inky cloak, good mother,

or customary suits of solemn black,

Nor windy suspiration of forced breath,

No, nor the fruitful river in the eye,

Nor the dejected haviour of the visage,

Together with all forms, moods, shapes of grief,

That can denote me truly. These indeed seem,

For they are actions that a man might play;

But I have that within which passes show:

These but the trappings and the suits of woe."

Kerry Blackstone was standing at the other end of the bar amongst a group of his admirers when he noticed something was happening. He excused himself and joined Gertrude and Culligan in time to pick up Culligan's cue line and deliver the King's response.

KERRY BLACKSTONE: "Tis sweet and commendable in your nature, Hamlet, to give these mourning duties to your father."

Gertrude said, "He says that he knows every line in Hamlet."

Curious, others from the company gathered, then fed cue lines to Culligan. He was able to provide the proper, though labored, response. Conversation with the company revealed that Culligan had never been on stage.

"Then how, and why, for God's sake, " Kerry said, "Did you manage to memorize all of Hamlet?"

"I was alone up in Canada for three years. Beginning with the first line in the play, I memorized the first lines, said them over and over until they were stuck in my head, and the next day I recited what I had already learned and committed more lines to memory. That way, by the end of three years, I had committed the entire play to memory."

Kerry Blackstone speculated. "While you've never been on stage, and your transitions are labored, to say the least, you have a good voice, you move well, you have presence, and you have no difficulty learning lines. With experience in front of an audience you could learn timing and become an actor."

Culligan shook his head. "No. You folks, you keep on doing the acting and I will keep on being part of the audience."

• • •

Culligan and Kerry Blackstone took to having their evening meals together. Culligan asked, "How did you come to be an actor?"

"My parents had a comedy routine. They were a filler act and played the music halls. By the time I could walk they put me in the act."

"Some advantage I suppose to starting young."

"Some advantages and some disadvantages. I developed stage presence, but also, I picked up the cheap tricks my parents used."

"So how did you become a Shakespearian actor?"

"When I was nine Robert Straley saw our act. He saw something in me and hired me to play Puck in 'A Midsummer Nights Dream.' He had me unlearn the tricks I had picked up, and taught me how to act. I was a handsome youth and when I was sixteen I began a two year run playing Romeo. We toured Britain, Canada and America. I have been in Shakespeare ever since."

• • •

Culligan became a favorite of the acting company. Their conversation sparkled, he enjoyed listening to them, and the 'Fair Ophelia,' transported herself to Culligan's bed. He had thought that Ophelia might belong to Kerry Blackstone, but it became evident that Kerry preferred the company of young men. Still, Culligan was impressed with Kerry's management of his acting company plus his accomplishments as an actor.

For his part, Kerry was fascinated by this wilderness man who had memorized the entirety of Hamlet, and he was more than willing to discuss acting. Once, Culligan went backstage and said to Kerry, "You did the "To be" soliloquy differently tonight."

Kerry admitted—"Yes, feeling something new; I went with it."

After each performance, the acting company would gather in the hotel bar to drink. Kerry said, "Culligan, you are not drinking."

"No, when I do drink, I sometimes drink a lot, enough to put any of you on your backs. I like strong drink too much, my mother was Irish, they drink too much, and so I usually choose not to drink. You people drink every single night. I can't do that."

What Culligan did not say was that, *although you all look good in your clothes, without clothing, your bodies look kind of flabby,* you eat too many sweets, too much soft food, and when I get close, you tend not to smell so good.

Culligan enjoyed every moment of having seen ten performances of the play Hamlet and almost every moment of having Ophelia share his bed. But, she was beginning to wear on him.

He bought a good saddle horse along with a packhorse, a spyglass, and rode out for Texas.

Chapter Eleven—Culligan's Return

Larco was comfortable doing the talking while Paul was comfortable with hardly ever talking. This worked for them. Cassy was their life, and the two men watched over her. She carried her own weight, but still, they watched out for her.

At the end of Spring roundup, with all the branding and castrating done, Larco, Paul, and Cassy sat on the top pole of the corral and watched as all of Swartzkoff's cattle were being added to the large herd being driven north.

As the herd was heading out and with the chuck wagon following, Old Man Swartzkoff rode back to say goodbye. "You two men knew nothing about cattle when you started and I thought you were too old for this kind of work. I have to admit you both are stand-up men and able hands. Cassy—not only do you stand and fight—I never saw a better hand at working a cutting horse. My years have caught up with me. This is my last cattle drive, I will be living with my daughter in Kansas City, and I wish you all well."

• • •

"Larco," Paul said, "this time of year, there is no chance that the three of us will be finding work on the same ranch."

Larco nodded, "There was that herd of wild mustangs we saw down by the border."

The three friends decided to round up those mustangs, break them to harness and sell them to the stage lines.

Cassy still believed Culligan would show up.

They bought supplies and headed south towards the Wheeler Creek area.

• • •

Culligan picked up their trail. He rode into Arlo on a good horse, and having a decent packhorse, good boots, a good hat, carrying his Avenging Angel in a belly-gun holster, and having a Winchester and a Sharps Buffalo gun in saddle boots. During those times, it was usually only those who lived outside the law who were this well-off.

For that reason, when Culligan entered a town he would begin his inquiries at the local Sheriff's Office. He tied his horse and packhorse up to the hitching post in front of the saloon and walked the short distance to the Sheriff's Office. The Sheriff was not in. Returning to the bar he ordered a glass of beer, some beef jerky and three boiled eggs.

Two cowpokes were sitting in the saloon. The stranger seemed to be paying them no mind . . . so they resumed their discussion of who was where in that part of Texas.

One of them mentioned, "Those three laid off from Swartzkoff's Ranch went through here and headed south. Larry Jenkins nodded and said, "My brother just came up from there, saw two niggers, one of them being a women, along with a white man, down on Wheeler Creek breaking some mustangs to harness."

One of them said, "Them's got to be the ones rode for old man Swartzkoff. Both the men will stand and fight and even the girl is said to be a good shot and will stand her ground."

The older cowboy said, "Those Circle J boys are not going to like this, not one damn bit, them getting first shot at those mustangs."

Culligan left the bar for the general store. He purchased beans and corn meal while the storekeeper provided him with directions on how to find Wheeler Creek.

Mid-morning the following day, Culligan reached Wheeler Creek. The question of whether to move upstream or downstream was cut short by the sound of gunfire coming from upstream. Riding along the ridge Culligan saw that his friends were being pinned down by fire coming from this same ridge and about a hundred fifty yards west of Culligan's position. From this vantage point, looking over the edge of the ridge, he saw that one man was working his way down and around to the south flank of Larco, Cassy, and Paul's position and another man was working around the northern flank while Peg-leg Walt Fipps and another man were keeping Culligan's friends pinned down with fire from the east ridge.

Culligan chambered the Sharps, put cartridges, one between each of the fingers of his left hand, and fired a warning shot close to the man on the northern flank. He rechambered the Sharps and the man turned to look in Culligan's direction, only to get shot in the chest. The second man had turned to look in Culligan's direction. Culligan rechambered and killed the second man.

Appearances count, and neither man had been backshot.

The two men on the ridge were caught in a crossfire between Culligan on the ridge and those from below. Peg-leg Walt Fipps was shot dead. Maybe it was just as well. He was sickly, always in pain, and didn't have much of a life anyway. The other man crawled backwards until he reached his horse and rode off. He was wearing a bright green coat.

Culligan hollered down, "That you down there Larco?"

Larco hollered back, "Sure is! That you up there Cully?"

"Sure is! Hold your fire while I ride down slow and easy."

Larco had a chunk taken out of his right ear but otherwise he was fine. Paul and Cassy were unmarked while Cassy was bouncing up and down what with the return of Culligan. Looking at her, Culligan said, "Cassy, you sure have grown up some since I saw you last."

While each of the dead men had small sums of money on them—the money was left in their pockets.

Paul Thrum's boots were about worn out and he was sorely tempted to exchange boots with one of the dead men. Cassy's saddle had also seen better days, but temptation was resisted.

• • •

Culligan rode into Arlo leading three horses with a dead man tied down across each saddle. The entire town turned out to gawk.

Cassy, Larco, and Paul Thrum herded the ten mustangs into the corral behind the livery stable.

Each of the dead men were known to those in the town—everyone knew everyone in that part of Texas.

Sheriff Eggers looked over the dead men, commenting, "They sure are dead alright." Turning to Culligan he said, "I have coffee on the stove." The Sheriff closed the door behind them and poured coffee.

Taking a cup, Culligan said, "I came through here three days ago looking for my friends Larco, Paul, and Cassy. I came by your office but you were gone."

"I know all that. Not that many strangers come through this part of Texas. We watch them close. What happened down there?"

"I found Wheeler Creek right where the storekeeper said. My friends were pinned down by fire from up on the ridge—that peg-legged fellow and one in the green coat had them pinned down—while the other two were working their way around to outflank my friends—I took a hand."

Sheriff Eggers rubbed the back of his neck. "Each of these men, including Heckle, the one that rode off, have friends in this part of Texas. You and those others you rode in with need to light on out of here or there's going to be trouble . . . and I already got more trouble on my plate than I have time to chew. Those mustangs, them being mostly broke to harness, I'll pay ninety dollars for the ten of them if you and you and those you rode in with will leave this part of the Texas pronto. That's not a real good price for those mustangs but that's the best I can do."

Thinking on the offer, Culligan replied, "I'll accept that for them. We'll be getting out of this part of Texas as quick as the condition of our horses will allow."

• • •

They rode westward while staying south of the border. Culligan picked up the bills, telling Larco and Paul, "This is pay for the two of you keeping Cassy safe."

Springtime they rode into Arizona. Cassy, Larco and Paul Thrum found work during spring roundup. Culligan left his horse and packhorse with Larco and on foot he explored the islands of stone sometimes rising up more than a thousand feet out of this sea of sandy soil and cactus.

Paul commented, "Seems to me the hooves of the cattle are tearing up what little hold the soil has. Most everything that grows here is hostile, either sticks to you or sticks in you. When the wind blows, dust devils rise up and almost blind you. "

• • •

By the end of spring roundup Culligan had returned. Sitting about the campfire with his friends, Culligan said, "That Catalina Mountain Range jumps strait up out of the desert. I found a spot where a trickle of water was coming down off the mountain and then sinking down in the desert. From the looks of things a good deal of water comes through there at some time during the year."

Larco's ears perked up. "Where is this place?"

"More or less," Culligan said, "about two miles north of the stage line road."

His three friends sat still, alert. Larco said, "You think a dam could be built where it would hold a decent pond of water?"

"I hadn't given that a thought, but thinking on it now, I think maybe so."

Culligan led the way, but once they arrived, he bowed out of any discussion on the land. It was up to Paul, Larco, and Cassy to consider the possibilities. They spent most of two days looking over the land and thinking on it. The land itself was poorly, but they found a spot where by building a five foot high and twenty foot long dam they could make a pond able to hold a considerable body of water.

Cassy and Culligan stayed put while Paul and Larco rode to Fulmer, registered a joint claim for the land, and with the money Culligan laid on them, put down an order for a thousand pounds of cement. Three days later, they arrived back at what was now their land.

Paul and Larco proceeded with building the dam. Cassy, now having a 410 shotgun as well as the Winchester, did the hunting and the gathering of firewood. Her hunting provided many a jackrabbit, an occasional deer, and she took to harassing the herd of eight javelina and the grandfather multi-colored gila monster until those creatures vacated the area. When the dam was raised to the proper height, and with a proper spillway, more stones were put in place on the face of the dam and spillway, more cement was mixed and the face of the dam and spillway received an additional coat of cement. In July the monsoon rains came and filled the pond.

• • •

Larco wrote to Hetty Baldwin.

Dear Hetty,
We done it. Paul and me we filed our claim. We have built our dam and it filled with water this monsoon season. We plan to irrigate, grow hay and vegetables next spring. It gets terrible hot in the Summer along with the monsoon rains. The Winter days are mostly dry and not too cold. Now that the dam is complete, we are putting up buildings. This is a large land and Paul and I will be building a large dwelling. This picture is of me and Paul. The nights do get lonely and Paul and I hunger for female company. It is my hope that you will hunt up someone who would be right for my friend Paul.
Larco

Chapter Twelve—Cassy and Cully

Culligan joined with Paul in finding more rock to strengthen the outside wall of the dam and spillway, while Cassy and Larco focused their attention on the manufacture of adobe bricks for the buildings to come.

The first adobe building was completed before winter set in. Garden plots and the means to irrigate them had been set. Windows and a cooking stove with an oven were ordered and paid for. Things were taking shape. Paul and Larco's heads were held high what with now owning their own piece of land.

Rolf Stanky from the stage line came by. He had heard that Paul Thrum was a man who knew horses and horseshoeing. After a day of discussion they came to an agreement that Paul and Larco would set up and run a relay station where they would provide a change of stagecoach teams. This arrangement would not only provide income, but also manure for their garden. Efforts were renewed to build a larger stable.

• • •

After a brief July monsoon, a pair of wood ducks showed up on the pond. Wood ducks live in the deep forest so how and why were they here? Probably the storm had blown them down off the Catalina Range.

Culligan said, "I know wood ducks from my time in deep forest. Wood ducks nest in the hollows of trees."

Paul Thrum built a box with an opening large enough for the wood ducks and hung it on a pole cemented in place. The pair of wood ducks found it to their liking and moved in. From that time on the pond and the property was known as the Webfoot.

• • •

"Cully," Larco said, "You ever climb that Catalina Range up behind us?"

"I have. Been to the top of the highest peak."

"What's it like?"

"Rough, twisty, steep. You can see the saguaro cactus forest where the Catalinas rise up out of the desert but higher up and between the peaks saguaro gives way to a woodland oak forest and a small pond. The higher peaks have pine forests at the top. I seen small green parrots up there able to get the seed out of a pine cone. Also, I found a canyon that has humming birds. Why that one canyon had hummingbirds while others did not, I don't understand. Once I stood on a foot high snowpack and looked almost straight down on Webfoot land that was dry as a bone."

"You ever climbing back up there Cully?"

"No. I already been there, already done that."

• • •

Cassy had been a child that Larco and Culligan protected. Now she was a woman and Culligan felt a need to protect her from himself. When his feelings heated up, him being a walker, he would pack a knapsack, pick up his Winchester, and say, "I'll be gone for a few days." Then he would disappear only to reappear from out of nowhere in maybe ten, maybe thirty days.

Culligan had been back for a few days, was lying on a knoll by the pond and watching the wood ducks going about their business while his friends were making more adobe bricks.

In the distance they saw what appeared to be a solitary figure riding along the wagon trail.

They could see that it was Frankie Ford, a good looking young black man riding the twenty miles out from the town of Fulmer. He was greeted friendly enough and invited to water his horse. Frankie asked, "Is that big Culligan fella still around?"

Larco answered, "He's probably up by the Webfoot looking on the water. He does that sometimes."

Paul cut to the point asking, "What brings you here Frankie?"

Looking directly at Cassy, Frankie Ford said, "I come here to visit with Miss Cassy for a spell."

Larco knew, Paul knew, and pretty much everyone knew, from the way Cassy looked at Culligan, that one day she would be his woman. With Frankie Ford having come courting, Cassy decided this was the time. Without a word she turned and headed for Webfoot Pond. Seeing this and embarrassed for Frankie, Larco and Paul dropped their eyes.

Frankie Ford hesitated, then started to rush after Cassy, only to have Paul and Larco jump in front of him. "Frankie," Larco said, "this day has been coming for a long time and now it's happening. Besides, you go up there now and Culligan will kill you for sure!"

"Not if I kill him first!"

"Not going to happen! Culligan is the best gunfighter ever! If he stays in this country someday someone looking for a reputation will backshoot him! It would be a good thing if Frankie Ford was still alive for Cassy when that day comes."

• • •

Culligan was lying on his bedroll watching the wood ducks. He had seen Cassy cross up over the dam so he was not alarmed when he heard her coming up behind him.

Then there was stillness and not a sound to be heard. He looked over his shoulder and saw Cassy standing twenty feet away and higher than him, with feet slightly apart and not a stitch of clothing. Sucking in a quick breath he exclaimed, "Girl, you have to know you are the most beautiful creature I have ever seen."

• • •

When Cassy and Culligan crossed over the dam and rejoined the others, it was clear.

Frankie Ford began the ride back to Fulmer.

"Culligan," Paul said, "You are a well-known gunman. Your reputation has protected Cassy from others, but it doesn't protect her from you, or you from her. I have seen you run away from her and I respect that, but she is so deep under your skin you can't stay away. You stay in this country and for sure someone is going to backshoot you. Then what happens to Cassy?"

"Those are strong words and the most I ever heard from you."

Paul nodded, "I am partial to you Cully, but I am more partial to Cassy."

The word spread that Cassy was now Culligan's woman.

• • •

The Reverend Beattie was not having a successful career. After each failed posting his denomination moved him further west and now he was posted to Fulmer. Learning of the affair between a white man and a black Jezebel, the Reverend Beattie recognized his solemn duty to visit the Webfoot and provide the spiritual guidance that the situation called for.

At dawn he harnessed his trotter to the buggy. Being a man of the cloth he rightly expected to be invited to spend the night at the Webfoot where his horse would be watered, fed and rested up for the return to Fulmer.

On arrival at the Webfoot the Reverend Beattie chose to ignore Paul and Cassy as he reminded Culligan and Larco of the Government's wisdom in having passed a law forbidding blacks and whites to marry. As a man of God Reverend Beattie informed them that Scripture made it clear that God disapproved of such unions.

Larco was amazed at the stupidity of Reverend Beattie and moved to stay between Culligan and Reverend Beattie; Culligan had grown too still.

For his part the Reverend Beattie was shocked at seeing hostility in the faces of the white men he had attempted to provide with wise counsel. He began edging his way towards his buggy.

Paul Thrum stepped in Reverend Beattie's way, unholstered his Colt, pulled down the hammer, and warned Reverend Beattie, "If you take one more step towards that shotgun I'll shoot you dead!"

Looking expectantly towards the white men, the Reverend saw there was no help coming from those two.

Paul then informed the Reverend, "There's about eight hours of daylight left. If you start walking now you might make it back to Fulmer before dark. I'll see that your horse and buggy get back to Fulmer alright, but if you ever set foot on the Webfoot again you're a dead man!" To help him on his way Paul fired into the ground close to the Reverend Beattie's feet.

As the Reverend scurried away he turned to look back. Paul again raised his pistol . . . and the Reverend turned back towards Fulmer.

• • •

The presence of Paul, Larco, and Culligan had always cautioned others to be respectful of Cassy. Now, thanks to Reverend Beattie, the early feelings of being disrespected slammed back into Cassy full force. Reverend Beattie had surprised Cassy and left her devastated.

Culligan walked about with head down and helpless to relieve the pain of this girl he loved—but he tried. "I could put you on a ship and take you to France." Unable to stop herself Cassy lashed out at Culligan, *"And what would you do then, sell me!?"*

• • •

Storm clouds were rumbling. Culligan then made what he later came to call, "The sorriest act and the biggest mistake of my life. When I lost my mother, wanting to be alone to lick my wounds, I packed up and headed west. Now having lost Cassy, I rode out towards Phoenix."

Traveling in the open and already in a foul mood, the monsoon rains landed on Culligan full force.

• • •

Months had passed. Culligan awoke with the recognition, finally, as to why Cassy had lashed out when he suggested putting her on a ship. The tales of the horrors of the slave ships had been very real to Cassy. He headed back to the Webfoot.

Chapter Thirteen—Serena is hospitalized

In the Summer of 1868, Earl Bates Sr. received Serena McNabb's weekly dispatch. Her report stated,

Dear Earl Bates Sr.

Upon arrival in New Orleans, I learned that William Culligan spent time in this city with a theatrical company that was putting on the play 'Hamlet.' I learned that Mr. Kerry Blackstone, who manages the company and also played the part of Hamlet, was presently in Baton Rouge. I interviewed Mr. Blackstone who reported: "You ask me about Culligan. He was with our company for a short time and our young actress who plays Ophelia shared his bed. Do not be surprised I know this. As Company Manager I keep a close watch on what each of my actors is doing, when, where, who with, and how many times.

Culligan amazed our company. He had actually committed the entirety of the play Hamlet to memory. This accomplishment, without ever having seen a production of the play, is truly remarkable. For ten nights he watched the play from a front row seat. After the play he joined with our company for our nightly drinking and socializing, bedded down our Ophelia, and then arose slightly before dawn to have breakfast and go off to do God knows what.

One of the irritating things a Shakespearian actor has to deal with is the playgoer who approaches us after a performance saying, 'I just love Shakespeare' while they don't know a damn thing about Shakespeare. Culligan never did that, yet when prompted, he was able to discuss the Shakespearean tragedies with logic and familiarity."

Knowing his background," Serena had said, I would not have expected Culligan to be a literate man, yet you say he is."

Blackstone had said, "A true diamond in the rough—but never-the-less a precious jewel." We in this profession have a low tolerance for being alone; we need our audience. Culligan, on the other hand, has a low tolerance for crowds. Following our last New Orleans performance, on the morning we were packing up to continue on our tour, Culligan came to bid us goodby—I have no idea where he might be.

• • •

Two weeks later, Earl Bates Sr. received a communication from New Orleans notifying him that Serena McNabb was in the hospital with a serious case of ptomaine poisoning—that the outcome was in doubt.

• • •

In his early years, Earl Bates Jr. had focused his attention almost exclusively on horsemanship and fencing. Surprisingly, since nothing good was ever said about his father, Earl Jr., at age sixteen, approached the father he had not seen since infancy, and asked him for a job. He was given a lowly job in the warehouse, asked for no favors and received none. Abruptly abandoning his excellence at horsemanship and fencing, Earl Jr. devoted his considerable energies towards work and learning the business. Each of his promotions were earned by dint of hard work and attention to detail.

By the time he was twenty-one, Earl Jr. was a supervisor and exercising his sense of responsibility and business judgment. At the age of twenty two, Earl Jr. was offered a junior partnership in the firm.

The Company's Letterhead then became Bates, Bates, and Collier.

• • •

With the beginning of the Civil War, Mister Earl Bates Sr. accepted a commission as a Supply Officer in the Union Army. In November of 1864, Earl Sr. was badly wounded and was retired from the Union Army.

His son, Earl Bates Jr. had been a dashing and daring Calvary Officer and personally, at his own expense, outfitted his company with Spenser carbines. Earl Jr. engaged in many bloody and decisive battles, yet came through the war with only minor wounds.

When his son entered his office, Earl Sr. said, "My boy, since you came home from the war you haven't been worth a damn for the business! My partner and I have waited for you to pull yourself together but it hasn't happened. Before the war you were as good as any I ever saw, but now you are a deficit in your present position."

Earl Jr. sighed while admitting, "It's true. I try, but I can't seem to get my head back in the business. The drive and the interest I had in business is gone, I don't know where it went, but it's gone. I was a good worker and then I became a good businessman. I was a good Calvary Officer, but now I flounder about and don't have a clue about what to do with my life."

Not unkindly Earl Sr. said, "While I don't want you in the business anymore, there is still something you can do for me, and for yourself as well. Take a seat son; I'm going to tell you a tale."

• • •

The senior Earl Bates told it all. Earl Jr. was dumbfounded, now having the history, finally, of his father's estrangement from the family. Earl Sr. reported, "I hired a remarkable young woman named Serena McNabb to look into this. She is now in the hospital in New Orleans suffering from a serious and possibly fatal case of ptomaine poisoning."

Earl Jr. looked up, but said nothing.

"Also, a detective has now succeeded in locating the daughter of the midwife who assisted in the delivery of William Culligan. The daughter preserved the records of those births her mother assisted.

Looking at the birth date of William Culligan, it became clear that he is my firstborn son. So there you have it. You have a brother out there somewhere."

"I have a brother out there . . . . . Did he serve in the Union Army?"

"I had accessed both Union and Confederate records and found no listing of a William Culligan. He spent the war years in British Columbia."

"Is he someone who runs away?"

"That he is not! Even as a boy he was known to stand his ground and fight. He is a loner and a gunfighter. I want you to go to New Orleans. Do everything you can to assist in Serena's recovery. If and when she recovers, I want the two of you to continue in the search for your elusive brother and my other son. If Serena McNabb does not recover, then I want you to continue the search without her. Can you do this?"

With an aliveness that had been missing for some time, Earl Jr. stated, "Yes Sir! This I can and will do!"

• • •

On arrival in New Orleans, Earl Junior's queries revealed that Dr. Redburn was the physician in charge of Miss Serena McNabb's treatment.

"In an effort to rid Serena McNabb of the poisons in her system, we put her through a series of purges. She grew weak, slipped into a coma and her heartbeat became weak and thready. All we can do now is provide her with baths, keep her warm and comfortable and provide small doses of nutrition when she's able to swallow. That and a wait and see attitude, are all that we can do at this time."

"Do more. Move her off the ward and into a private room, provide me with a reclining chair along with the means to spoon-feed her when she's awake and able to take nourishment."

• • •

Serena became aware she was being moved to a private room. Move accomplished, she fell asleep. She awoke to see a man resting in a reclining chair in her room. Aware that she was awake he arose and came to her bedside saying, "I'm Earl Bates Jr. My father sent me to look after you and see that everything possible is done for you. You need to take some of this broth."

Serena took four spoonful's before shaking her head indicating she could do no more. Mostly, she slept. Each time she awoke Earl Bates Jr. was there.

Growing stronger and more alert, able to eat more, she recognized that Earl Bates Jr. was tall, slender, and the handsomest man she had ever seen.

Serena grew stronger and Earl took her for carriage rides about New Orleans. The two of them pored over the reports on Culligan.

Earl was hopeful when he reported to Serena, "I found a newspaper report of a gunfight on Wheeler Creek in Texas where a man named Culligan killed three men. The newspaper stated the killings were justified and there is no call for Culligan's arrest. Time-wise, we are getting closer to Culligan."

"Earl," Serena said, "that was months ago. He could be a thousand miles from there by now."

Earl muttered, "Um . . . Serena, you seem to think you know Culligan, and maybe you do . . . are you in love with this elusive brother of mine?"

"I've never met the man. When I do I might be repulsed as I know he is a hard man. But yes, I think I am in love, at least, I am in love with the image I have of this man. Only time will tell!"

"Serena, you are attractive, intelligent, and most desirable, but under these circumstances, I think we would do well to maintain a brother and sister relationship, at least until such a time as you actually meet this elusive brother of mine."

"Thank you Earl. We'll be traveling together, and I didn't know how to bring up the subject, but you are quite right and I am profoundly grateful."

Chapter Fourteen—Culligan is Shot

Two middle-aged women, one white, one black, were traveling together from Belting, South Carolina. Loren Smith, tall and black, was subjected to some small slights. Hetty Baldwin, shorter, slender, and white, while in Belting, had held her tongue even though it had pained her to do so. No more! She took umbrage and spoke her mind at any slight to her companion.

The two women arrived at the Webfoot by stagecoach. Neither woman had met Paul Thrum. What they knew of Paul was the picture they had seen of Paul and Larco plus what could be gleaned from the letters dictated by Paul, written by Cassy, and read by Hetty.

Larco took Hetty's hand as she stepped off the stage.

Paul cleared his throat. He said, "Miss Loren," offered her his hand, she took it, and stepped off the stage.

Seeing each other for the first time, both Paul and Miss Loren were speechless, and what a moment that was.

Cassy was standing off some distance and leaning into the shelter of Frankie Ford's arm. They came forward, introduced themselves, and Cassy said, "The outhouse is out back."

• • •

"Frankie and Cassie," Larco said, "will be fixing dinner, Paul and me would like to offer you our arms and show you around the Webfoot."

Hetty said, "We want to see Webfoot Pond." Loren and Hetty, seeing the pond, looked at each other and heaved a sigh of relief.

Loren said, "The soil in your garden and hayfield looks poorly and not like the soil in Belting . . . I should not have said that."

Paul turned to face her. "Miss Loren, here on the Webfoot, you say whatever you have a mind to say."

• • •

Loren was speechless at being set down at the table. Halfway through the meal she looked to Paul, saying, "Sitting down to eat with white folks—other than Hetty—this is a lot to take in."

Paul nodded, "First time I saw Culligan and Larco here with our young Cassy, I couldn't believe it. When I saw they really were friends, it made me dizzy. I had to grab ahold of a hitching post to keep from falling over. Here on the Webfoot, this is our world here—and a different world from what you and I ever knew."

Larco spoke up. "Paul, you and me, we been partners going on three years, and in all that time not once did I hear you string that many words together. Miss Loren, you being here has turned my partner into a gabby sort of a man. Why in no time at all, you might even get him to smile or tell a joke."

After dinner, Paul and Loren went for a walk up by the Webfoot. When they returned at dusk Loren said, "This is where I want to be."

• • •

Sheriff Shoup had served in the Confederate Forces as a Sergeant. After the war, traveling west, his proficiency with a gun was noted. He was elected as Fulmer's Sheriff, and had done what others thought of as a good job of keeping the territory free of Mexicans.

Since it was thought by most that Mexicans would be there only to rustle cattle, when Sheriff Shoup caught a Mexican north of the border, even if they hadn't rustled any cattle yet, it was believed that in time they would, so why waste time? He hung them anyway.

Sheriff Shoup said, "There had been those niggers Paul Thrum and Cassy showing up and staying. Then Frankie Ford showed up.

I thought then that things were getting bad.

Now, with this Loren Smith showed up and moving onto the Webfoot—it's clear that this is just the beginning and unless we do something, it is only a matter of time before the territory will be crawling with niggers. We need to do something."

• • •

Culligan, waking up, came to the full recognition of how Cassy would have recalled tales about the horrors of the slave ships. This recall had been triggered when Culligan suggested that he put Cassy on a ship. He thought, *I should have stayed to fight for this girl.*

On his heading back towards the Webfoot, in the shallows of a creek-bed, Culligan saw a school of minnows. On riding into Fulmer, Abe the bartender informed Culligan that Cassy was now married to Frankie Ford, that Larco and Paul Thrum had each taken a wife, and that Sheriff Shoup intended to put a halt to what he called, "this invasion by niggers."

Culligan rented a horse and buggy along with a ten gallon barrel and returned to the creek having minnows.

• • •

Those on the Webfoot saw him coming. When Culligan pulled up to the Webfoot, Paul, Larco, and Frankie Ford were standing with their wives and waiting to meet him. Cassy came forward saying, "With the look on your face when you left I thought I would never see you again—I married Frankie Ford."

Nodding, Culligan said, "I did you a disservice. I'm older than you and I should have stayed a father and not bedded you. That was not right. And my leaving when you were hurting, that was not right either.

"The folks in Fulmer were quick to tell me you were married. Cassy, I want you to know I meant you no harm when I said I would take you to France. I want you to know that."

"I know that now." Sighing she said, "It's for the best; I knew it even then. If we'd stayed together you would have had to shoot half the white men in Arizona. My husband is a good man but he is jealous of you and what we were to each other. I beg you Cully, please don't hurt my husband."

Again, nodding that he understood, Culligan reminded Cassy that she should probably be getting back—that Frankie needs to see you move away from him and back to Frankie—he needs to see that. Cassy stepped back and Culligan called out, "I remember you Hetty. You keep that man on the straight and narrow, you hear." To Paul he said, "You going to introduce me to your lady?"

• • •

Culligan said, "Lets get these minnows into Webfoot pond while they're still alive."

The minnows were set free in Webfoot Pond and Larco fetched up a gallon jug of Thunder and Lightening. Larco, Paul, and Culligan stretched out by Webfoot Pond and proceeded to get drunk.

Larco said, "Robert Stanky, the agent for the stagecoach line, told me that rancher Sandy Cresto has his eye on Webfoot water and the stagecoach contract that goes with it. He said that Sandy Cresto is the one behind Sheriff Shoup's efforts to run us off the Webfoot."

Paul said, "Both Sheriff Shoup and Deputy Acuff have suggested we might want to move on. I told them we were staying, that we have womenfolk to look after, and we're staying."

Culligan put down the jug. "Anything happen so far?"

Paul nodded. "I was out riding when I saw the glare of the sun dancing off the barrel of a rifle. Bailing off my horse, I avoided being drygulched and I found tracks allright. Deputy Sam Acuff has small feet and the boot tracks I found could have been those of Sam Acuff.

Culligan thought on it. He said, "My Remington's been traded in for a New Army Colt conversion to 44 caliber cartridge and with the barrel cut down. Paul, you think you could scare me up a spent 36 caliber ball?"

. . . "I might be able to do that."

Paul and Larco looked at each other. Larco said, "Cully, you planning on doing something about this?"

"Deputy Sam Acuff carries two Navy Colts in 36 cap and ball with butts forward cross-draw style. You two and Frankie Ford have womenfolk to care for. I don't have that responsibility—not anymore—I failed Cassy once already. I might do something about this . . . I just might. Larco, you take this packet, bury it somewhere. Don't dig it up unless you men need to take up the women and move on and Paul, I'll be needing a 36 lead ball."

• • •

Culligan stood at the far end of the bar. It was this time of day that Sheriff Shoup and Deputy Acuff usually entered the saloon. He knew that coming into town, Sheriff Shoup would have been warned that Culligan was in the bar. He figured that the Sheriff would enter through the front door while slippery little Deputy Sam Acuff would enter through the back.

He was right. Rancher Sandy Cresto and Sheriff Shoup, talking loud, entered through the front while at the same time Deputy Acuff slipped in through the back door and out of bright sunlight into the dimness of the tavern. Culligan had expected this. Culligan and Acuff both fired, with Culligan's shot took the Deputy in the chest while Culligan took Acuff's shot in his neck on the left. The shot missed the jugular and exited below his left ear. It was not a dangerous wound but it was a bleeder. At the same time Sheriff Shoup and Sandy Cresto went for their guns. Culligan shot them both dead.

Culligan reloaded, rubbed his hand against his bloody neck and then rubbed his hand against the right side of his chest as if he had been shot in the chest. He said to the bartender, "Abe, you got a bar rag or something I could use to stop the bleeding on this neck wound? The other's not bleeding much, at least on the outside."

Abe gave him the only clean bar rag he had and Culligan faked two coughs. On the third cough he spat out the lead ball preserved in his cheek. The lead ball clattered on the bar and in the silence it could be heard rolling along.

For the rest of his days Abe insisted he had actually seen a lung-shot man cough up a lead ball.

The town's storekeeper proclaimed, "That is plain foolishness! It was from the neck wound. The lead ball got lodged in his throat and he coughed it up!"

No one disputed Culligan having coughed up a lead ball and it was too good a story to be let lay . . . It traveled. What was disputed was whether it was coughed up from a lung wound or the neck wound.

• • •

Mounting his horse, Culligan was able to make it to the San Pedro River. His neck wound had stopped bleeding . . . finally.

The wound was not all that painful, but he had swallowed blood from the inside, lost blood from the outside, and was weak and close to fainting. Still, he tethered his horse, laid out his bedroll, put his bloody shirt in the river, anchored it down with a rock, and let the running water wash out the blood. He bathed the caked blood off his hands and body and rolled into his bedroll.

• • •

The next day, word of the gunfight had traveled by stagecoach to the Webfoot.

Cassy was much distressed on hearing that Culligan had been shot in the neck and chest and then had coughed up a 36 ball.

On hearing this last report, and remembering Culligan's request for a spent 36 ball, Paul and Larco looked away from each other to keep from laughing.

Paul was a man not given to humor. He enjoyed the humor of Larco and sometimes smiled when with Miss Loren. Otherwise he was a solemn, quiet sort of a man. It was suspected that until Paul met Miss Loren he had never smiled. Having heard from the stage driver that Culligan had been shot in the neck and chest, then having coughed up a 36 ball, then having mounted his horse and rode away, even Paul was having difficulty keeping a straight face.

After the team of fresh horses were hitched up and the stagecoach had passed out of earshot, without looking at Paul, Larco muttered, "Do you suppose?"

Paul responded, "So it would seem. I think so."

The two friends could not hold it in any longer. They started laughing and the more one of them laughed the more it spurred the other to laugh. Their laughter grew so out of control that soon they were hiccupping, gasping for breath, and had tears running down their leathery cheeks.

Frankie and the womenfolk were bewildered. They could not see the humor in Culligan having been so badly wounded. Seeing their bewilderment then spurred the two men to fresh laughter. Larco could not open his mouth without laughing so it was up to Paul, between gusts of laughter, to explain the trick Culligan had pulled.

It was agreed; if Culligan wanted others to think he was so tough he could cough up a lead ball, then none on the Webfoot were going to say different. Culligan was not in the territory, but even so, the image of Culligan had a long reach.

• • •

Rancher Sandy Cresto had been making noise about running for Governor. Governor Case was not sorry to learn that Sandy Cresto was dead, and would not sign a warrant for Culligan's arrest.

Word arrived that Culligan was recovering and resting in a room above a Cantina south of the border. Cassy took it in her head that she needed to go see Culligan. Frankie was uneasy about Cassy visiting her first lover, but with Culligan so wounded, he was left with no choice. Larco would go with Cassy, and Frankie and Paul Thrum would stay behind to protect the womenfolk and the interests of the Webfoot.

• • •

When Larco and Cassy crossed into Mexico and rode up to the Cantina, they were recognized as friends of Culligan and greeted hospitably enough. On entering the Cantina the owner simply pointed to the stairs and said, "Second door from top Senorita." At the second door Cassy knocked twice and said, "Cully?" Hearing her voice, Culligan said, "Wait a minute." Cassy heard Culligan grunt as he rose from his chair and made his way to unlock the door. When the door opened Cassy saw a pale and wan Culligan. He was letting his short beard grow another inch to cover the neck wound. Cassy began to cry and moved into his arms. After being held for a time, Cassy moved out of his arms and Culligan returned to his chair. The wound was healing but the trip into Mexico had weakened him.

Cassy sat on the edge of the bed and watched as Larco entered and grasped Culligan's hand. He offered the opinion that Culligan looked like he might live after all. Culligan agreed and said he was getting a little stronger but he was probably going to continue resting up for another week or maybe longer.

Larco noted, "There were some who swore that they saw you being lung shot and then cough up a lead ball. Others seemed doubtful, saying that this does not seem possible and maybe the lead ball got stuck in your throat. So far no one has voiced the thought that it might have been some kind of a trick."

"It was a trick allright. I faked being lung-shot but you don't need to tell anyone. I figured if I was going to get myself shot up I might as well get some fun out of it."

"Well," Larco said, "you sure did get them talking and at the moment, no one seems interested in giving us trouble! The idea that you are out there somewhere, and that you could return any time, makes others think twice about coming after us. You are now as famous a gunfighter as John Wesley Hardin and Wild Bill."

"All the more reason for me to get out of the country— which is what I intend to do. What about you folks?"

Larco nodded, "With the freight line and the stage line stopping for a change of horses, we have horse manure to add to that poor soil, and we've got the irrigation set up for our garden, Paul knows about gardening, so does Loren, and we grow our own vegetables."

"What about rabbits and deer?"

"We got two hounds that keep them and the coyotes on the run. While we're making a little money now, what with providing water, some blacksmithing and a change of horses for the stage and freight lines, that won't last. The railroads will eventually come in and freight and stage lines will lose out, so we brought in a few head of cattle. Mines are opening up all over Arizona and with people moving in to work the mines, the call for beef will get high."

Quiet through all this, Cassy grew restive and said, "Larco, I want to see Cully alone and you will allow me this."

Larco nodded, shook Culligan's hand and said his goodby. He left and closed the door behind him.

Cassy said, "You did this for me didn't you."

Culligan was quiet for a moment. "When I saw you in the water alongside that lifeboat—and with you helping me up on the beach—then waking up finding you giving me water, washing my face with fresh water, I vowed to myself that I was going to help this girl. I thought to be a father to you but you grew up and were so damn beautiful I lost my way. My being almost 20 years older, it was my responsibility, not yours, and I did you a disservice by bedding you. You being married now, it's best I be moving on."

Cassy nodded, "I think so. Frankie is a decent man and it makes me happy being married to my Frankie. I think of you every day Cully. I didn't have a life. You came along and gave me my life. Frankie Ford gave me my name, which is something you could not do. Now I am Mrs. Frankie Ford. Other than my name, everything else I have came from you. Will I ever see you again?"

Culligan hesitated, "Probably not. Mostly, I kept my head down about the gunfights but with this last one, the stunt I pulled, even here in Mexico people are talking about it. So, there will be men out there wanting to be known as the man who killed Culligan. Still, we could leave people thinking I could be back any day."

Cassy laughed, "They already think that. We say, Culligan is sometime gone for a few days, sometimes for a month and then you wake up and he's there. He says, 'Everything all right, folks treating you right?' Then he's gone again. We tell them that no way could we have a better friend than Culligan. Where will you go Cully?"

"I'm not one to sink my roots down deep, but I been thinking about when I got off a ship in Panama. Panama stays warm year round and I don't much like cold. When I got off the ship I decided to take my time crossing the Isthmus of Panama. I went for a walk in the jungle and enjoyed seeing the birds and plants and other animals.

"Still, the trees there crowd in on you. I prefer open spaces where I can see who or what is coming. I don't much like being caught out in the cold come winter and I hear there are plenty of warm open spaces in East Africa and Australia. I intend going to Sacramento, then pick up the money I have there, and then I'll be heading out for London by way of Panama. Then I'll probably head for either Africa or Australia, which ever comes first.

"I will always carry in my head a picture of you from that time I saw you standing there naked by the Webfoot. That was the most beautiful sight I ever saw and one I'll never forget. That Frankie Ford is the luckiest man alive."

Cassy's eyes filled with tears. She leaned over and kissed Culligan, first on the forehead and then with a firmer kiss on his lips. Then, straightening up to leave, she said, "I'll always love you Cully."

• • •

Cassy closed the door behind her. Culligan listened as Cassy paused, then strode down the stairs. Culligan stayed still for some minutes . . . then he got up, locked the door, and returned to his chair and the book he was reading.

Chapter Fifteen—To the Webfoot

Larco received a letter from New Orleans. It's author was Mister Earl Bates Junior.

Dear Mr. Larco,
I am the half-brother of William Culligan, the half-brother he never knew he had. I too never knew I had a half-brother. There can no longer be any doubt that William Culligan is the son of Mary Culligan and our father, Mister Earl Bates Senior. My associate, Miss Serena McNabb, is presently recovering from a serious illness.
In the near future, after she grows stronger, Serena McNabb and I will begin our journey and you may expect our arrival at the Webfoot.
We are desirous of meeting with this elusive half-brother I never knew I had.
Respectfully,
Earl Bates Jr.

• • •

Larco said, "That letter sticks in my mind . . . who are these people? Is this Earl Bates really Cully's half-brother?"
He looked to Hetty who said, "Could this be real or could it be

people found out Culligan is a rich man and want a cut of the pie ? When they get here we need to look at them real close."

Larco agreed, raised his hand and said, "We don't tell them anything unless we are sure."

• • •

The stagecoach carrying Earl Jr. and Serena pulled into the Webfoot around midday. Their long ride across Texas and New Mexico, the desert heat and roughness of stagecoach rides had taken their toll. It was recognized that Serena McNabb was at the end of her strength—Hetty promptly took Serena's arm and steered her to the outhouse and then to the room and cot that had been prepared for her arrival. Gratefully, she sank down on the cot while Hetty removed Serena's shoes, and loosened her clothing.

• • •

After some hemming and hawing, Larco asked Earl what might be the relationship between him and Serena?

"At the moment it's pretty much a brother and sister relationship. Serena is looking me over but she is more than a little curious about my half-brother Culligan. After we meet with this brother of mine, she may make a choice, but until then, it will remain pretty much a brother-sister relationship."

Larco wagged his head from side to side. "Never even met the man, yet already he's reaching into her life. He does that. But you get too close and the next time you look up—he's gone—."

• • •

Earl had been grateful for the chance to get off the stagecoach and stretch his long legs.

After getting Serena settled, Hetty returned outside. Earl said, "Is Serena all right?"

"She seems to be resting comfortable.

Earl nodded. "We should have taken more time for Serena to rest before beginning the trip, and taken more stops to rest, but knowing of Culligan's proclivity for moving on, if he was on the Webfoot, we had hopes of catching him before he left."

Larco nodded, said, "That makes sense."

"I would like, Earl said, to wait until Serena is able to join us. Then we'll tell you all we know."

• • •

Earl looked over the dwellings, the stable and the dam. Seeing the vegetable garden and the watering system devised for the garden and hayfield, Earl nodded in approval. The chicken pen had 10 hens and one strutting rooster. All in all, Earl noted that the Webfoot and its buildings and dam had been carefully laid out and new constructions were underway with considerable care.

Previously, Larco had been the best cook. Gratefully, he had surrendered up the kitchen to Hetty and Loren.

It was late afternoon and the sun was setting on the western horizon when Serena awoke and rejoined the others. A meal of batter-fried jackrabbit, chicken, boiled vegetables, cornbread and pinion nuts had been prepared and Cassy had discovered wild peppers growing not far off. Garlic and onions had been grown and salt, pepper, bay leaves and cinnamon had been purchased.

When the meal was finished and the dishes were put to soak, everyone returned to the table—they waited for Earl to explain why Serena and he were there.

Earl cleared his throat, "This is hard to talk about. My father loved and intended to marry a young chambermaid named Mary Culligan. While my father was out of town on business, the woman who was to be my mother, along with my grandmother, convinced Mary Culligan that my father had only been toying with her and that he intended, on his return, to marry the woman who later became my mother. They either did not know or did not care to know that Mary Culligan was pregnant, and they drove her away. When my father returned my grandparents told him that Mary Culligan had left in the company of a prosperous older man. Disillusioned, my father married my mother-to-be. Father learned the truth of Mary's leaving only after my second sister was born.

"Meanwhile Mary Culligan had traveled to New York City and given birth to a child she named William. She supported him the best she could until she was murdered 14 years later. When my father learned the truth of what my mother and grandparents had done, he moved away from my mother and grandparents and has refused to speak to them since that day. It was too late to make amends to Mary Culligan. By the time father learned of the offenses committed against Mary Culligan, she was already dead.

"Efforts to locate Mary Culligan's son were fruitless. William Culligan had disappeared.

"By chance, some years later, my father learned that a man named Culligan was known to have been in California. Detectives were again hired and traced William Culligan's movements up and down California and Western Canada. Investigators were never able to determine his present whereabouts, only where he had been. They learned that Culligan had traveled to Panama and then disappeared one more time."

Earl cast his eye on Cassy and Larco. "Later, we received a report that a man who might be William Culligan was seen in Louisiana traveling in the company of a young black girl and an older white man."

Earl chose at this time to turn his look on Serena. "My father also learned of the exploits of a Union spy named Serena McNabb. She was reported to be an astute judge of character and had a knack for figuring out what others could be expected to do next. None of the previous investigators had demonstrated any success in anticipating Culligan's next move. With this in mind, father sent for Serena McNabb. Shortly before her arrival he learned that William Culligan had returned to New York and had stood at the grave of Mary Culligan for more than three hours. The following day he visited his old neighborhood, then took the ferry to Fort Lee, and disappeared again." Earl then looked to Serena.

She said, "I was hired to locate and speak with William Culligan. I followed him to New Orleans and learned of Culligan's association with you folks."

"Before Serena could proceed further," Earl said, "she became ill and almost died of ptomaine poisoning. I was dispatched to join her at the hospital in New Orleans. When she recovered and was able to travel, we came to the Webfoot. So here we are. We are looking to meet with my half-brother, my father's firstborn son."

"Perhaps," Serena said, "you would like to take time to think about this, to come to some agreement as to how much you are willing to help us in locating the son of Mary Culligan. I am afraid I will need to rest before continuing. I'm not as strong as I had thought and we are able to pay. My present weakness means haste in coming to a decision is not necessary."

Earl placed a stack of reports on the table. "These are all the reports we have on William Culligan. Read them if you must, but help us find my half-brother. Our father is ill and wants to meet his first-born son before he dies."

Husbands and wives huddled for much of the night discussing this.

• • •

The following morning all gathered together for a cautiously pleasant breakfast. During the meal Cassy and Serena continued to exchange looks with each other. When breakfast was over, Cassy said to Serena, "If you're feeling up to it we could go for a walk."

Serena said, "I would like that." The two women walked silently past the dam and to a spot where they could sit and enjoy the view of Webfoot Pond. Serena broke the silence between them saying, "We gathered that you once had a relationship with Culligan and then he left you. Is this true?"

Cassy was silent for a moment. "Not quite. I drove him away. I'm married to a good man now, and I would never betray my husband, but Culligan gave me my life. Culligan taught me to ride and shoot and mostly he taught me to hold my head up high. He taught me how to read and speak something other than Gulla. I love Culligan more than you can imagine. "This spot, where we're sitting now, is the exact spot where Cully and I first made love. It may surprise you to know that even though he is a rich white man he loved me. It was me pushed him away—I could see the hurt in Cully's eyes—I hated it, but even then I knew that it was for the best, that if he stayed someone would have backshot him. Under all that hardness he is a good man. He is long gone but I could never have a better friend than Culligan. He gave me my life and everything I have except my married name."

Cassy paused for a moment and continued, "I suppose you find it strange to think that a strong, rich, white man, one who could have whoever he wanted, would love a poor black girl like me."

Solemnly, Serena said, "At first I did, but then I thought more on it. You are an intelligent and brave girl, you love Culligan, and you are gorgeous. Thinking on what I know of this man I should not be surprised that a free-thinking man like Culligan would not hesitate, even you being black, to fall in love with a remarkable young woman like you."

Cassy took some time to soak this up. Then—after a pause—Cassy turned to Serena and quietly said, "What about you? Are you in love with him?"

Serena looked back, took her time and replied, "I'm not sure. I've not met him, but I feel I already know him, and if not Culligan, then I will probably marry Earl Bates."

"He seems decent enough. Also," Cassy said, "he is the handsomest man I ever saw."

"Ah! You noticed."

The two women laughed together and then spent time chatting about various topics including the two wood ducks and their four chicks going about their business on Webfoot pond. After a time Cassy mentioned that they needed to be getting back. Friends, the two women strolled back hand in hand, laughing and enjoying their shared secrets. When they were all together, Cassy looked to her husband and friends and said, "I think we should do all we can to help these people find Cully."

For the first time, Serena and Earl Bates had more than a history of where Culligan had been—they now had information as to Culligan's future destinations. Rather than attempt to follow Culligan to Sacramento, Serena and Earl decided to travel to San Diego, take a ship to Panama, and wait for Culligan there.

• • •

Arriving in Panama City, not the prettiest or the safest city in the world, Serena and Earl took separate rooms in a good hotel conveniently close to the docks. They met every ship that docked.

On a humid and hot August afternoon, Earl Bates and Serena McNabb had stationed themselves at the dock where a ship had begun disgorging its passengers. Moving easily with a suitcase in one hand and a rifle case in the other, was a tall, broad shouldered, and vigorous appearing man.

Serena intercepted him and asked, "Excuse me sir. Are you William Culligan?"

Culligan lowered the suitcase, surveyed the scene and those about. In particular, he kept his eye on Earl Bates, who looked to be someone able to handle himself. Earl was tall, slender, and weighted about 160 pounds. Culligan was tall, broad, and weighed over 200 pounds. Earl recognized he was being sized up and turned his hands palm up. He cocked his head to one side as if to say, "*See, my hands are empty.*"

Caution was necessary as Culligan was carrying a large sum. Having surveyed the scene and seeing nothing to alarm, but still cautious, Culligan asked, "And if I am?"

Serena replied, "My name is Serena McNabb and this is Earl Bates Jr. His father is also your father. Your father has been looking for you for a long time."

Culligan didn't speak.

Serena continued, "It was your friends on the Webfoot who let us know you would be coming through Panama. They made it possible for us to meet you face to face."

Putting this together with what he already knew, Culligan said, "Will Pennypeck told me that private detectives had been running up and down the Coast looking for me. Tell me the name of your hotel and I'll meet with you in the morning."

After learning the name of their hotel, Culligan, carrying his suitcase and riflecase in his left hand, strode off. The revelation that he had a father who was intent on meeting with him stirred up a well of emotion. He searched for, and found, the Valdez Commercial Bank.

Culligan informed banker Arturo Valdez that he wished to convert funds into English pound notes.

Arturo Valdez noted that men exchanging large sums of money usually exuded an expansive mood. This man seemed almost distracted, not really focused. Arturo said, "Perhaps your trip did not agree with you?"

"Culligan refocused, opened the suitcase. It contained a minimum of clothing, three boxes of cartridges, a holstered long-barreled

Army Colt Conversion to 44 cartridge, and the rest of the suitcase was filled with stacks of money.

A cashier was called in to count the money being converted to English Pounds. Their business was completed and the banker recommended a nearby hotel for the night.

• • •

Early the following morning, Culligan circled around Serena and Earl's hotel. He detected nothing that was cause for alarm. Still, he entered the hotel through the door to the kitchen rather than through the main entrance. He trooped through the kitchen, entered the lobby, and Serena and Earl started to rise. Culligan motioned for them to remain seated, took a lobby chair with his back to the wall and facing the two of them, he waited for Earl Bates and Serena McNabb to explain themselves.

"My father," Earl said, "was in love with Mary Culligan. He told me how your mother loved good books, theater and long walks. She had been a chambermaid in my grandparent's home. When father was away on business, my mother-to-be and grandmother lied to your mother and drove her away."

"The one time," Culligan said, "that I asked mother about my father, Mother told me that she had loved him, but she had been tricked, driven away by two conniving bitches, and that my father had also been tricked. Mother said that by the time I was born my father was married to one of those bitches. Mother said that the one good thing that man did was give her a fine son."

Serena looked to Earl and said, "A noble woman and mother."

"What my mother and grandparents did," Earl Bates said, "is unforgiveable. Mary Culligan was already dead by the time Father discovered the lies that drove your mother out of Boston."

Earl Bates continued, "I despise the offenses enacted against your mother. When I went to work for father, mother laid down an ultimatum that I would have to make a choice between either her or my father. I do not like ultimatums and chose Father."

Culligan nodding, unthawed a fraction.

"Knowing," Earl said, "as I do of the injustices and the humiliations heaped on your mother I can well understand that you might wish to do my mother harm. Culligan, I know that your usual way of dealing with offenses committed against you or your friends has the ring of finality. I suspect every man you shot was trying to shoot you. However, you are out of your depth with my mother, so leave her to Father. Mother is in for an unpleasant surprise."

Culligan's eyes blazed, he opened his mouth to speak, then deciding, he gave a brief nod, was still curious, but didn't ask.

Earl reported, "I'm feeling drained by all this. Finally meeting the brother I never knew I had . . . .. If you two will excuse me I have to write a report to Father. Then I would like to take the two of you to lunch."

Alone with Culligan, Serena said, "He has not told me what your father has planned for his wife, only that he does have a plan and that it is a beauty. We've been on pins and needles, anxious to meet you, and fearful that we might already have missed you. Now that we have that worry out of the way we can relax a little. I think I'll take a nap. Earl likes to eat at around twelve, so perhaps you could meet us here in the lobby at that time?"

Chapter Sixteen—Vengeance

At twelve noon Serena, Earl, and Culligan met in the lobby and went for lunch in the exclusive hotel restaurant.

The table with its multiple setting of different forks and spoons was beyond anything Culligan had previously experienced.

After having lunch, and while having coffee in the salon, Earl said, "I assumed you would have difficulty in selecting the right fork or spoon to use, yet you sailed through without error."

"When one of you would pick up something I picked up the same. The same dish you addressed was the one I took on."

Earl chuckled and Serena said, "Even the waiters may have assumed you were familiar with this setting. Culligan, how and why did you memorize the entire text of 'Hamlet, Prince of Denmark'?

"I love the language of Shakespeare. Hamlet is a favorite of mine because he is constantly looking inward and giving expression to the contradictions he finds in himself."

They saw Earl's eyes go big. Serena said, "What?"

"My brother loves language, his mother loved plays and our father contemplated becoming an actor before being called on to take the helm of the family business."

Serena listened as Earl and Culligan discussed theater. Things these two very different brothers shared in common was the love of good theater and good writing. Earl listened with rapt attention as

Culligan reported his conversations with Kerry Blackstone on the art and craft of acting. Earl was led to say, "You think you could play Hamlet on stage?"

"I could not. Night after night having to deal with the indecisiveness of Hamlet would drive me to drink. I like strong drink too much, and that is why I seldom drink.

"Kerry Blackstone assured me that Macbeth is the best of all Shakespeare's plays. Earl, you have the looks and your indecisiveness about what to do with your life could find full play in the role of Hamlet." Shaking his head, Culligan said, "I'm more like Claudius— I kill first and feel guilty afterward."

• • •

Culligan said, "I spent my first fourteen years in New York City. New York looked down on my mother and then it killed her. After losing my mother I took myself away from New York and those people as fast and as far away as I could get. But there was no escape. The injustices I saw in New York were pretty much what others suffered in California."

"Such as?" Serena said.

"Indians being hunted for their scalps to make doll's hair is one example."

"I know that gold was found on Sutter's land," Earl said, "and I know Sutter was squeezed off his land. When your mother died, you headed out west."

"Losing my Mom, I needed time to be alone and that was the right thing to do. But when I thought Cassy was lost to me, rather than stand and fight, I headed out, and that was the sorriest act of my entire life. But still, it turned out allright for Cassy, with Frankie Ford being a decent young man, and now she thinks of me more like a father, not a lover. But my leaving her the way I did—that was not right."

Earl had an additional thought. Later that evening he said, "Cully," if you don't stop beating on yourself for leaving Cassy, if you don't let that go, settle down, marry Serena and have a family, you will die all alone out in the wilderness."

Culligan thought, nodded, and said, "That is probable."

• • •

Culligan, Serena, and Earl traveled by carriage across the Isthmus to Colon. From there they booked passage on a ship bound for New York City. Culligan went armed, always, with the Avenging Angel, but there were also times he arrived at the ship's rail with a long-barreled New Army Conversion holstered on his right hip and with the butt facing forward. He practiced fast-drawing the longer barreled Colt with each hand, pulled back the hammer, and stared down the barrel at the sea.

"Cully, Earl asked, "what are you doing?"

"The newspapers are digging up all they can find on Culligan the Gunfighter. They are ranking me up there with Hardin and Wild Bill. We are being rated the top three and there is speculation on who would come out on top if we were to face off."

"How would you fare against those men?"

"I can prepare for that but if I stay out in the west, for sure, I will get backshot."

"After meeting with my father I am heading for London and then for either Africa or Australia. In the meantime I look out to sea, make note of a little piece of foam or flotsam on the water, draw the Colt, pull down the hammer, and keep my sights on that piece as the ship rolls and heaves."

• • •

In the dark of night Culligan stood alone at the ship's rail. Serena joined with him . . . she cleared her throat. "Reading the reports I had on you, even before meeting you, I was in love with you. If I were stranded on a desert island with one man I would want that man to be you since I know you would keep me alive."

"You and Cassy you are the only two women whose company did not wear on me with the coming of daylight but I was not right for Cassy."

"You are not right for me either— unless something changes you—makes you ready to settle down."

Culligan took her in his arms and kissed her. They stood at the rail holding each other.

• • •

Once they had disembarked in New York, Earl Jr. sent a telegraph message to his father informing him that he would be arriving with Serena and Culligan on the next train to Boston. When the train arrived, Earl Bates Sr., looking pale, wan, and leaning on his walking stick, waited on the platform. Exiting the train Serena and Earl held back so as not to intrude as Culligan and Earl Sr. took in their perceptions, each of the other. Earl Sr. clasped Culligan's hand with his, saying, "My boy!"

• • •

In the days that followed Earl Sr. excused himself from the conduct of business. His body was still carrying lead, and some of that lead was apparently moving about and causing mischief. Still, there was time for Earl Sr. to express his regret that Mary Culligan never had the chance to know how much he loved her and that losing her was the saddest day of his life. Earl Sr. stated, "I wish she could have known!"

"She knew!" Culligan said, "Molly Bannion had worked in your mother's kitchen, and she told my mother that it was your mother and the woman you later married, who tricked you. My mother learning of this, it comforted her to know your love had been true!"

Earl Bates Sr. staggered. Culligan and Earl grabbed their father to keep him from falling.

Serena and Earl Jr. kept company with each other and observed. They did not often intrude when Culligan and his father were together. Earl said, "In a way I'm envious. My father is dying, but even so, he looks at peace with himself and even happy. The father I knew seemed distant and somehow detached from everything but business. All those years— and I never realized how troubled and sad he was."

• • •

Earl Bates Sr. called them together. "I have little time left. Having now met my firstborn son and knowing that Mary Culligan knew it was not me who betrayed her, I am ready for this. While Serena was recuperating from her recent illness I hired the most prominent attorney in Boston to draw up a new and air-tight will."

Earl Sr. extracted from his desk drawer three identical legal packets, handing the first to Culligan, the second to a dumbfounded Serena McNabb, and the third packet to his second son Earl Bates Jr. "In this, my last Will and Testament, I have left my share of the business and this house to my long-time friend and business partner William Collier. Also, I have designated Serena McNabb as my adopted daughter.

"Upon my death, the bulk of my estate will be divided into three parts. One part will go to my adopted daughter Serena McNabb, and a second part will go to my son Earl Bates Junior. Mister William Culligan, your present wealth exceeds what you will inherit. Therefore, I have left the home where my wife presently resides, plus the third part of my wealth, to Mister William Culligan, *and with the stipulation* that Mr. William Culligan will set this Inheritance in a Boston account and allow my estranged wife to reside in that house until her death. My daughters abandoned me but I will not abandon them, not completely. They and my estranged wife will receive their copies of my Will on this day. A copy is also being retained in the possession of the attorney who drew up the Will.

"My estranged wife and daughters may receive funds from this account *only at the discretion* of my first-born son William Culligan, who is already a man of means."

Twenty-eight days later, Earl Bates Sr. succumbed to the effects of his wartime wounds.

• • •

Such events are supposedly sad—this was not—the three of them were there, and Earl Bates Sr. was pleased on seeing them as he slipped away.

After the funeral, Mrs. Nancy Bates approached William Culligan and reminded him that she was accustomed to being maintained in a certain style and she was quite sure that her late husband intended that she be maintained in that style.

Culligan responded, "I'm sure. When my mother's employment was terminated, the severance pay she received was fourteen dollars. Is that correct? "

Haltingly, Mrs. Bates stammered— "I believe that is correct."

Culligan took money out of his pocket and counted out fourteen dollars.

Mrs. Bates looked at the money and gasped out the words, "I can't live on that!"

"Neither could my mother. To support me, she had to turn to prostitution. If you can not make it through this month on fourteen dollars then I suggest you do the same.

"Next month, and every month after, you will receive enough money to live on if you are frugal and do your own cooking. Of course, you will not afford a cook or servants. Your daughters will receive word that *upon your death* the home will be sold and the moneys, plus the money in my Boston Account, will then be divided equally between your daughters, but only on your death."

Nancy Bates was stunned and speechless. Pale, she staggered from the room.

Culligan thought, *this payback may not be all she deserves, but at the moment it feels pretty damned good.*

• • •

Chapter Seventeen—To Africa

On a foggy day, Miss Serena McNabb, Captain Earl Bates Jr. and Mr. William Culligan, arrived in London. The local Society Column took note of their arrival and that they had taken rooms in London's finest hotel. The next day the bellboy presented Serena with a sealed note. Earl, watching, said, "Bad news?

"I hadn't known how I would deal with my family. This letter resolves the question. My father has reminded me that I will receive no financial support from him."

"What are you going to do?"

"Nothing. I am now a wealthy woman and soon enough he will recognize that he will receive no financial support from me."

• • •

Culligan noted that London's upper classes were buzzing around the three of them like houseflies.

Shooting tournaments had been held in Bisley Park since the Fourteenth Century and archery had now given way to pistol and rifle competition. Culligan placed well with the Sharps rifle. In the handgun he was placing with the leaders. One of them noted. "You are shooting with factory-issued grips and factory sights. The rest of us are shooting with custom fitted grips and target sights. With custom grips fitted to your hand and target sights you would probably have the advantage of us."

"Perhaps." He then shifted the long-barreled Colt Conversion to his left hand for the next round of shots. "This, plus the heavier charge of the 44 cartridge, is the advantage I choose to keep."

• • •

Back in New Orleans Culligan had met Timmy Oats, a lisping young man who was Kerry Blackstone's dresser. Now in London, in the theatre lobby, Timmy recognized Culligan, was delighted and effusive in his greeting, and after Kerry had made his last curtain call, Timmy corralled Culligan's party of three and ushered them backstage to the dressing-room of Kerry Blackstone.

Kerry's eyes lit up seeing Serena accompanied by Culligan, "So," he said, "You did find him, I am glad. Allow me, after I've taken off the makeup and am out of costume, to take the three of you to dinner at the most exclusive restaurant in London. It's always helpful for an actor to be seen with the best people."

• • •

Kerry Blackstone took pleasure, Serena being a writer, in introducing her to those in London she would do well to know. He also spent time discussing acting with Earl Bates. Culligan asked Kerry, "How would Earl do as an actor?

"Earl reads intelligently. He has a good voice, good carriage, is even better-looking than I was at his age and I'm going to introduce him to a fine director. If Earl is willing to listen, Director Bishop will turn him into an actor."

• • •

Serena traveled to the Mediterranean shores of France and Culligan accompanied her. Like Culligan, Serena did not like the cold winter. She located a one storied house with a good well, garden, grape arbor, and stable overlooking the Mediterranean shore and retaining a middle aged couple to cook and maintain the property.

Jaques and Eloise were older, slightly overweight and even after having raised three grown children they were still passionate in their love for each other. They had assumed that Serena and Culligan were sleeping together, and it saddened and puzzled them, to realize they were sleeping in separate rooms.

"Serena," Culligan said, "when my mother died, I went for my first long walk. When I lost Cassy, I went for another walk, but not as long. Now my father has died. I don't know why, but I have to do this. I'll be shipping out for Cairo on the Fifteenth, and then I'll probably go up the Nile to the Sudan. Eventually I will get this long walk out of my system and then I'll be back."

"William Culligan, all my life I have had to cover up what I thought and what I felt. No more! You are a bastard to leave me like this! You go take your damned walk! I'll wait for you no more than eighteen months. If you do not return ready to settle down by that time then I am going to ask Earl to give me a child. Mister Culligan, you ask one hell of a lot of a woman! Now get out of my sight! Do not let me see you again until you are ready to settle down!"

• • •

In Port Sudan Abraham Leibowitz saw the white face of Culligan swimming in a sea of black. He called out. Culligan said, "I don't speak French."

"Ah, an English. Come, let us drink together."

"Maybe I will." Culligan entered the establishment of Abraham Leibowitz, dropped his backpack to the floor, and sat.

"This how you do business, corral passersby you think might have a dollar to spend?"

"Absolutely! White men, other than seamen in search of strong drink or the Port's prostitutes, are seldom seen in this part of town. But first let us drink together.

"Seeing a white man passing through with a pack on his back and armed, I make it my business to find out if that man intends to go into the interior, maybe to farm or prospect. Any of those is an opportunity for me to do business."

"You speak the language?"

"I speak two of the more than a hundred. Plus, I speak Arabic. We have almost 200 ethnic groups in Africa, each is struggling for dominance . . . or for survival. The situation is always in flux. One needs to recognize this if one is to survive. Your survival offers me the opportunity to do business with you. Incidentally, how did you get here? There are no ships in the harbor at this time."

"I caught a ship to Cairo, and from there I caught a ride to Alexandra. I walked down the Suez until I came across four Arab seamen who would be sailing an open boat for Port Sudan. I jumped at the chance to travel in such a craft. Those seamen really knew what they were doing. I know a few things about seamanship but not a candle to what those fellows are capable of in open water. When we landed in Port Sudan, it being mostly Muslim, I couldn't find a drink anywhere. Then you offered me a drink . . . .. How is it that a white man, speaking French, plus English with a French accent, ended up here in Port Sudan?"

"I had been a member of a French Expeditionary Force sent up the Nile to the settlement of Atbara. From there," Abe said, "We had orders to explore and map the lands to the west, a land known as Chad. My being a Jew, I had no future in the Army. Also, when I saw these tall, beautiful black women I thought, *this is what I want.*"

"So you are a gentleman of the Jewish persuasion."

"No persuasion—was born to it. I deserted and headed east and when I arrived in Port Sudan, I visited the ships in port. I traded, I bought, I sold. My wife Fatima, is beautiful. My daughter Zimah is beautiful and my sons Matak and Samir are strong young men who wish to visit the interior, in search of what I cannot imagine."

"What is out there that would attract?"

"What you will find out there are prides of lions, packs of hyenas, baboon colonies, poisonous snakes and tribal wars."

"Not a hospitable land."

"Not. What I left out are the Arab slave traders. They are better armed, though not as well armed as you, and they are dangerous."

• • •

Abraham and family lived in back of the store. He said, "My daughter Zima is 16 years old and looking on you with favor."

"I noticed. I am older, but no question Zimah is beautiful and if I were to stay in this land then I would be looking on her with favor. At this time all I want is to take a walk in this land and when I get that out of my system I may choose to stay in this land or I may return to France."

"You are well-armed and are used to a solitary life in the wilderness. I think that you are also a wealthy man but you are restless and want to keep moving."

"Abraham, only one other man ever read me that well—he too is a storekeeper."

• • •

Culligan bought supplies and began walking. He crossed the Nile at the settlement of Atbara and headed west through the Libyan Desert, staying well north of the more populated grasslands to the south.

Culligan was traveling alone through the seemingly waterless barren tracts to the west. The French Expeditionary Force he encountered was having trouble locating water. When they encountered Culligan, it seemed to them that Culligan had a source of water. The Officer in Charge asked where they could find water?"

One might say Culligan was not exactly friendly with those soldiers. He did not turn his back on them and when they were out of range, he continued walking west.

• • •

Chapter Eighteen—Slavers

One evening Serena, on returning from her walk along the Mediterranean shore, saw a large man sitting on the steps, beside him sat a tiny black girl in a yellow dress.

Culligan was back.

When she grew closer she saw that he was thinner, but there was something else that was different about him. It occurred to Serena that he looked comfortable, at least with himself. She thought, *Only Culligan could be comfortable at returning while bringing with him a young black child.*

Culligan and Cheruni stood. On Serena's arrival she looked closely at the girl. She was young—no more than seven years old—the girl interrupted her stillness with quick looks to Culligan. Turning to Culligan, Serena commented, "I waited a year for this? I didn't know you would arrive with a daughter."

"Adopted," he said.

"I have a letter. It's from Hetty. I'll get it"

• • •

Serena opened the letter.

Dear Serena,
Miracles do happen. I am 45 years old and yet I just gave

birth to a healthy baby boy. Larco and I are happy with this. Also, Cassy is with child. In this territory the stories about Culligan grow taller every day. People in this territory take pride in having been acquainted with someone so tough he could cough up a lead ball. A whisky salesman, hearing this tale, nodded and said: 'Up in BC, I heard from someone who saw it, when a man backshot Culligan, the lead ball skidded along his skull, took some bone along with it, then Culligan turned and shot the man dead. We knew that story was wrong, it was Jeremiah got shot and then Cully shot the backshooter; but still, Larco nodded and said, "Sure sounds like Culligan." Culligan is a legend that does not die. That legend has grown even bigger than the Man.

All of us miss him.

Hetty

• • •

Once Culligan had digested Hetty's letter, and Serena again had his attention, she ushered him and Cheruni in and prepared a repast of sliced pears, a loaf of bread, mustard, a cheese plate, and a carafe of lemonade. On seating herself, Serena said, "I heard whispers coming out of Africa, rumors that you had 'gone native' and were sleeping with African women." With a warning note in her voice she continued, "Now you tell me the truth and this better be good!"

"The truth is . . . those black women and even the men are a beautiful people and I liked them about as well as any people I ever met, maybe more, but not much more. Mostly I kept to myself."

"Once I met up with four young Sudanese men. I had shot an antelope and had more meat than I could use so I invited them to eat with me. After we ate that antelope, they had a little discussion and decided, using gestures, to invite me to travel with them to the west. Since they knew the land and where to find water, and I was going in that direction anyway, why not. On a morning five days later we arrived at a small isolated village. I counted thirty huts.

"We were welcomed and the women and children found me a curiosity. They ran their fingers through my hair and beard and rubbed my skin to see if the color would come off. One of the women reached up inside my shorts. Evidently she found I was put together like other men and what she found met with her approval.

"Towards evening me and the young men I came in with got together in the center of the village. We started good-natured tussling with each other and showing off to the young women who were circling and watching. Those women were wearing a band around their waist and another band around their forehead and that was all. They were a handsome people. The largest of the men I came in with was Butu. He gestured for me to come and tussle with him, so I stripped off my shirt, the belt with the long-barreled Colt, Butu didn't have shoes so I took mine off, but I kept the Avenging Angel in my waistband. My butt was closer to the ground than Butu's long legs would allow and he couldn't move me. I was sort of embarrassing him so I let up and allowed him to throw me to the ground. I landed flat on my back and laughed. I could see in his eyes that he understood what I had done and he was grateful. I reached up from the ground, Buto took my hand, and I pulled him on down. Everyone, including Buto, laughed. We were even and we were both laughing with the sheer pleasure of it.

"It was getting dark. Then, the drums started to beat. My friends all knelt down on one knee. I did too. Five young women entered the center and began to move to the slow, sensuous beat of the drums. Working themselves up, their bodies twitched as the feelings hit them. The light of the campfires flickered off their bodies now glistening with sweat, and in that light they were a glorious sight. I realized what this was about; why the men had traveled so far from their own village.

"The drums stopped and each woman made her choice by placing one leg across the shoulder of the kneeling and chosen man. I was chosen by the tallest, and I think the oldest, of the women. She was 17 or 18 years old, tall, slender, and with a beautifully chiseled face. After my being chosen I gathered up my gear and she took me by the hand and led me to her hut. I think this was a small village that understood the dangers of inbreeding. They needed new blood each generation and on the following day each of the women would be married to someone from their own tribe.

"The next morning Butu and his friends headed back eastward. I continued westward."

• • •

"One morning," Culligan said, "before the sun heated things up, I was wiping the morning dew off plant leaves and rocks for drinking. For food I had locusts and termites. That day and in that hot barren land I was eating termites. It was still. There was not a sound outside the buzz of insects and I began hearing in my head a chorus of musical strings pulled tight and humming. The sound rose and filled my head and then it mellowed and was gone.

"In the stillness that followed I asked myself, *'What in the hell am I doing out here when I could be comfortable with Serena in France?* By that time I had walked near half way across Chad. I had kept moving all my life just to get away from the pain of losing people I loved. I sort of hurt and couldn't stand being around anyone for long without becoming either irritated by them or downright angry with them. That day it came to me that I did not hurt, I wasn't mad anymore, and I didn't need to keep moving on.

"I guess my not being angry started with Cassy and Larco helping me out of that boat and up on the shore. I woke up to Cassy wiping my face with fresh water and she gave me drinking water. Later, she gave herself to me. That mellowed me out a lot more. Leaving Cassy was my fault, not hers. I can't blame anyone but me. Meeting my father took away most of my anger but the sorry part is—I never noticed it was gone—all that was left was the memory.

"I thought, maybe I can stop with the moving on. Then I started on my walk back to you."

"You," Serena said, "walked away from me almost a year ago and now you come back expecting me to be waiting? Amazing. So you think you have no need to keep moving on. That may be true, but I am not so sure."

"I thought, I'm ready to settle down."

"You think."

"I thought. Then I came across something that needed being done."

"Oh God! I am beginning to think there will always be something that needs being done."

"Cheruni was all alone in that desert. She would have died if I hadn't adopted her."

"Uh huh. And you do not wish to talk about the something that needed being done? Like I said, you ask one hell of a lot of a woman! Are you sure you didn't bring any diseases home to me?"

"Couldn't. There was only the one and she was a virgin."

"How lovely for you!"

In the descending evening dusk, the three of them ate the rest of the sliced pears and cheese. Serena lit a lamp, rose from her chair and said, "Cheruni, come." With lantern in hand she took Cheruni for a tour of the house, opening drawers and showing her everything including the Chamber pot under the bed where Cheruni would spend the night.

Having assured herself that Cheruni was settled in for the night, Serena came into Culligan's arms and said, "This could be the biggest mistake of my life. You sure you did not bring any diseases home to me?"

"That I'm sure."

"You know I am a virgin."

"I know."

"You are a smug bastard Mister Culligan."

"I know."

They embraced in a long kiss. Culligan hooked his arm under Serena's knees and raised her in his arms. She laid her head on Culligan's chest and he carried her into the bedroom.

• • •

Serena's virginity had been a burden carried too long. She was shy but also eager to shed that burden and not at all deterred by her mother's warnings about discomfort— surprise—no discomfort. In fact—it felt damn good.

Unlike her mother's grim silence, Serena was loud and the sounds of their lovemaking reverberated. Passion for the moment spent, and stillness having descended, Cheruni quietly entered the room and climbed into bed with them; she was scared being alone in a strange land. On this night, they did not object. Early morning they sent her off to her own bed.

• • •

When Eloise arrived to cook Serena's breakfast, she saw Culligan's pack and heard the sounds of lovemaking coming from Serena's room.

Eloise, humming, began preparing a breakfast for two. It pleased her to see Serena, followed by Culligan, coming out of the bedroom. Turning her head, Serena said, "Cheruni. Come." Seeing Cheruni come out of her room, Eloise gasped, then returned to the kitchen to prepare a third breakfast.

After breakfast Serena said, "That was quick. We consummated our relationship, I became pregnant that first night, and in the morning I delivered our first child. I am aware that someday you may leave me, and then it will be my responsibility to raise our child."

• • •

Chapter Nineteen—Scotland

Serena had sold several of her short stories, completed a novel of 60,000 words and a book of poetry. The novel did not satisfy her, nor did it satisfy Culligan.

"It appears to me," Culligan said, "that your writing is good, moves well in the beginning but then it bogs down in the middle because your heroine turns *nice*. She needs to do like you did. When I told you I was going for another long walk, you were not weak, not nice, not long suffering. You flat out told me that unless I was back and ready to settle down in a certain time then we were through. In that middle section your heroine needs to be strong like the Yankee spy you once were. I reread that middle section. Something has to happen there—a gunfight, someone cheating on his wife, a miscarriage—something has to happen and your heroine needs to deal with it."

Serena thought on it, then exclaimed, "Ah! I knew it was not right. . . . of course. It needs something . . . not a gunfight, cheating or a miscarriage, but something where my character is tested. I'll work on it. Thank you Cully."

• • •

"Serena," Culligan said, "should we be getting married?"

"I thought about that, thought that if you came back we could live together unmarried. I have money now, you have more—we could spend the winter months on the Mediterranean and return to Britain in the summer months. With my family learning of my living with a notorious gunfighter in an unmarried state, it would embarrass them, and that would please me. Also, scandal would call attention to my writing. But you arrived bringing Cheruni and that changes things. Now, especially if you ever leave Cheruni and me, we have to be married.

"When we arrive in Briton I can introduce Cheruni as my adopted daughter. Cully, you fail to appreciate that Cheruni is a girl that likes pretty clothes. I am taking her to Marseilles to shop for clothes. Ivory bracelets will do nicely on those lovely arms. I will become Cheruni's mother and you have already become her father. As much as I would enjoy scandalizing my parents and brothers, for the sake of Cheruni, we need to marry."

• • •

Culligan located an estate in Scotland that had suffered financial losses. "Serena, they want to sell out, cover their losses, and start over in Australia."

One thing Culligan liked about the estate—it had a plateau, a Rocky Butte sticking straight up in the air about 400 feet. Culligan appreciated the Rocky Butte. Climbing it would keep him strong. He said, "I don't know a damn thing about living in a mansion with servants . . . how to manage it."

"True."

"So. You will teach me the things I need to know."

• • •

Culligan learned that Captain Selky, who owned the largest estate in the area, was being openly critical, laughing at what he saw as the folly of this fellow Culligan. "He has no idea what he is doing. He thinks that buying that poor McCulloch estate will make him a gentleman. Everyone knows the pastures have been overgrazed and are worn out. This Culligan fellow even has the temerity to introduce a black child into this community."

The innkeeper, John Phillips, was someone Culligan liked, and someone who reported to Culligan what he heard.

A month after moving in, Culligan hired every unemployed craftsman and laborer in the area for the estate's much-needed repairs.

• • •

Earl Bates traveled from London to be best man at his brother's wedding. Cheruni was the Maid of Honor. Serena and Culligan were married by the local Priest in the local chapel—eyebrows raised—but more in curiosity, in surprise, than in condemnation.

Consideration of Serena's growing literary reputation, plus Culligan's reputation and his wealth, made it fashionable to say, "Oh yes, we have made the acquaintance of the writer Serena McNabb and her husband Mr. Culligan. The girl they adopted from Africa is quite lovely."

• • •

Time had passed. On this day, Culligan was overseeing the loading of all his sheep; they were being shipped by train to buyers up North.

Captain Selky, now having an audience who would observe him putting this American upstart in his place, said, "In the recent American Civil War, other American men honored themselves by demonstrating great valor. Tell me Mr. Culligan, why did you choose to avoid participation?"

"When I bought this estate, I decided to get rid of the sheep. The fields have been overgrazed and it will take a century, if ever, for these fields to recover. Sheep are pretty much like foot soldiers. They stand undecided and go nowhere unless directed . . . put a goat with a flock of sheep, the goat will decide to move, and the sheep will follow. Goats are almost as dumb as sheep, but at least they can decide to move, frequently in the wrong direction, but sure of their own wisdom . . . pretty much like Military Officers."

Captain Selky barked, "See here! I have led men in battle on two continents and have never been wounded. That should tell you something!"

"It does. In the West, when a particularly dumb goat would lead the sheep into harms way, the wolves would do their best not to cut down the goat that had provided them with such easy pickings. I am the best. I have been the lone survivor in 17 gunfights. Still, even I have been wounded. You, I look at you and I see a man slow and unsteady of hand and foot, a man whose vision is cloudy. I am left with the conclusion that when the shooting started you were the man who was not there."

All were silent and listening, some dropped their eyes, possibly in embarrassment, perhaps amused, but all holding their breath, waiting to see where this was headed.

Captain Selky opened his mouth but before he could speak, Serena cautioned, "Be careful. My husband is the wolf. Each of those seventeen well-armed men who came after my husband are now dead."

• • •

Back in London Earl was playing small parts and some not-so-small parts while studying stagecraft. He had a flair for comedy, something that eluded both Serena and Culligan, and he was the handsomest man on the London stage. Since he was willing to play small parts and with small pay, he worked all the time.

Earl was forewarned of the dangers of letting the visit to the tavern after every performance become part of his lifestyle. Earl needed little warning. Unlike his older brother, who had an Irishman's love of strong drink, Earl did not care for liquor and Earl allowed for visits to the saloon only after opening night and the last night's performance of the play. The other nights he adjourned to a coffeehouse.

• • •

It was a windy and rainy Fall day when Cheruni, Serena, Earl, and Culligan gathered in Kerry Blackstone's living room. They were served coffee and biscuits. The servant was obviously offended by having to serve Cheruni. Seeing this, Kerry placed his hand over Cheruni's and said, "James, Alfred could use some help repairing that hedgerow. I realize the weather is unpleasant, but change your clothing and go assist Alfred. When the repair is completed, something Alfred assures me will take at least ten days, then you may return to in-house service. In the meantime we will struggle along without your attitude. You may go."

After the servant James had exited, Serena exclaimed, "Well! That was brutally efficient."

Kerry nodded and said, "Also necessary." Kerry Blackstone sighed, "I will be spending more time on my estate now that I have grown older. When I was young, I was the handsomest man on the English stage. This opened doors for me but it was not enough. I wanted to be the best actor possible and that required more than looks and the usual actors tricks. I worked hard. Every word, every gesture, every thought and feeling, was thoroughly analyzed. I studied my craft."

Earl carefully sat down his coffee cup, turned to Kerry and said, "That thoroughness is what I am striving for."

"And just now you demonstrated that. You set down your cup, then turned to me, and delivered your line precisely. Each move was economical, decisive, and clear. You have an actor's instinct and timing. You will get there my boy; you will definitely get there.

The upcoming theatre season will be my last playing Hamlet."

All were still—Kerry continued, "Earl, you are not yet ready to play Laertes, but like Laertes, you too are a man of action and in time the part will take you in and by the end of the tour you will be a credible Laertes and I will know whether you are ready to play Hamlet." Kerry looked at Culligan.

Serena saw this and said, "You are looking at my husband as if afraid to ask."

"Quite right— Culligan, do you have any desire to be an actor?"

"I do not. But, if the tour were to travel to Vancouver, B.C., I could pick up the money I have there. If Serena and Cheruni are willing, we three could travel with the company."

Kerry stated, "Your proposal that we tour Canada intrigues me. You would be credible as Claudius and could double as the ghost. I am going to turn in for the night. You know the way to your rooms. Tomorrow we can start making plans."

Chapter Twenty—Culligan's Guilt

For three weeks Kerry Blackstone cajoled, threatened, bullied, and otherwise taught and rehearsed Earl in the part of Laertes. Earl had worked as an actor steadily for the previous two years. While his skills, his presence, and his natural charm might have been enough to satisfy his audience, they were not enough to satisfy Kerry Blackstone. He pushed Earl to the point of rage—or tears—and brought out the best in him. With Culligan, he cajoled, leading him towards the well of guilt Culligan did not want to face.

The day came when Kerry threw his hands up, satisfied, and said, "The teaching is over. It's time to assemble a cast and begin rehearsals."

• • •

The company began their tour in Inverness, Scotland. Earl, as Laertes, had moments of brilliance, Culligan was credible, not brilliant, but credible.

"Earl," Kerry said, "will never stop striving for more. I can see it coming. By the time we conclude our tour, Earl will be a fine Shakespearean actor."

The engagement in London received decent reviews and the company then shipped out for Quebec, Canada.

• • •

Montreal was where it happened.

For the first time, Act Three, Scene Three came alive. As Claudius, Culligan knelt to pray for his sins, but could not. The guilt of Claudius for the murder of his brother that Kerry had been reaching for, arose, captured Culligan, then the audience, and lit up the stage.

The scene built to a climax. The last two lines of the scene were,

My words fly up, my thoughts remain below.

Words without thought never to heaven go.

The moment was more than words; they were felt with deep emotion. The curtain came down, and applause arose.

Looking at Culligan, Kerry said, "Now my friend, you are in touch; now, you are an actor."

Seeing this, Serena was worried. Culligan said, "Damn! I feel like getting drunk but I won't."

"Cully," Serena said, "what happened out there on that stage?"

"For that moment, I was back in Africa."

"You ready to talk about it?"

"Not yet."

• • •

The actors in this company were an articulate, gregarious lot. They were delighted with Cheruni and she with them. In their company, Cheruni's vocabulary and social skills soared.

Serena watched how the audience responded to everything that happened on stage. As a prelude to playwriting, she looked to see what worked and what did not.

Now in touch with his feelings, Culligan was electric on stage. However, this awareness was not what he wanted. But, because the company needed him as an actor and as someone useful to have at hand when they collected money from the box office, he hung in.

By the time the company reached San Diego, all had money, all were tired, and all were ready to give it up. The Canadian and American tour was an artistic and financial success, the actors were paid off, and went their ways. Culligan, Serena, and Cheruni would return to Scotland by way of Panama.

• • •

In the open carriage leaving Panama City, Cheruni and Serena looked left and right, while Culligan , staring straight ahead, saw only what was in his mind's eye. Serena said, "You walked through here, and then you met Larco."

He nodded. "If Larco hadn't been on that ship, in that lifeboat, and Cassy had not been on that shore and fetched me water, I would be dead. My having now become a landed Scotland gentleman I will never see either of them again . . . and that is a damn shame."

• • •

In Scotland, in June, they received a visit from Major Edward Straight and Miss Jeanne Gerrard. The Major said, "I intend to lead an expedition from Quito, Ecuador across the Andes Mountains to those rivers running East. I will require the services of four well-armed foot soldiers who will be traveling with us."

Looking to Miss Jeanne Gerrard, Culligan said, "And you?"

The Major answered for her. "Miss Gerrard is a teacher by profession and a purveyor of ancient documents, searching church records, she made a remarkable find and has acquired a map detailing the locations of the seven cities of gold the Spanish discovered as they sailed upriver. I have agreed to lead an expedition to relocate those cities of gold. It is my understanding that you have experience at grubbing for gold."

"I would not call it grubbing. But yes, I have found gold—quite a bit of it."

"One thing I will not tolerate is any of my Expeditionary Force taking up with native women."

All looked to Culligan. For some moments he did not speak. He turned to Serena. "Serena my Dear, would you ask Maisy to pack a lunch for our guests? I think they might enjoy having lunch in the gazebo up on the Butte. It's cooler, more comfortable up there."

Keeping a straight face, she said, "Why yes my dear, I think that would be quite lovely."

• • •

Culligan was provided with a large picnic basket, and led the Major and Miss Gerrard to the path up the Rocky Butte. That path, initially, gave no hint of how brutal it would become. Culligan said, "I think I'll run ahead and set up lunch in the gazebo."

The narrow, steep and shale-slippery path would not tell them how far they had traveled or how close they were to the top. Culligan's guests reached the top in a half hour. Culligan had laid out lunch on the gazebo table, and had been engaged in target practice."

The Major did his best to not indicate his exhaustion while Miss Gerrard, younger, made no effort to disguise her fatigue. Her lips and legs were trembling and at the moment she was too nauseous to eat.

Culligan said "You folks intend to carry your supplies up and over the Andes?"

Major Straight said, "That would not be necessary. I intend to hire porters to carry our supplies."

"You are going to hire porters to carry your supplies through a jungle where by taking two steps off the path, the porters and your supplies would disappear from view. Huh . . .. Let us have lunch."

"Mister Culligan," Miss Gerrard said, "how willing are you to commit yourself to such an undertaking?"

"Years ago I might have undertaken such a journey, yet with the sure knowledge that most of you would be dead before we reached our destination. At that latitude leather rots out quickly and you would be barefoot even before you reached the Andes. Your clothing would rot out and by the time you crossed the mountains, if any of you were still alive, your clothing would be reduced to a rag between your legs."

Miss Gerrard, exhausted as she was, evidently saw some humor in the image of men being reduced to having only a rag between their legs. She chuckled.

Major Straight grew apoplectic. "How dare you, Sir, say such a thing in front of Miss Gerrard!"

"Actually," Miss Gerrard said, "on learning that I had acquired this map, Major Straight imposed himself on me, insisting he was the one to lead this expedition. I have gone along with this so far, looking to see where it would lead."

"Where it will lead is getting you killed."

Major Straight said, "See here!"

"Miss Gerrard, if you go through with this, I suggest that you start here in Scotland, put a pack on your back, load it up and walk with it at least six hours every day. . . Get a canoe and paddle every day and let your hands grow thick with calluses. Get as strong as you possibly can. Get a large caliber revolver and learn how to use and care for it. Only after that, go to Quito. Then take time to know the jungle. Only when you know the jungle, do you cross the Andes, either alone or with one man, a man who knows the jungle and who you can trust."

"I see," Miss Gerrard said, "I don't think I can make it down off this Butte. Will you help me down?"

"Do you intend to take this trip through the jungle?"

"I do not."

"Then I will help you down."

"Thank you. I am an explorer of documents, not jungles. A hard lesson you have taught me Sir."

Chapter Twenty-one—The Lone Wolf

Masoud had been troubled. Each passing year the number of his goats lessoned. It was his responsibility to provide for his wife and their five children. In his youth, more than 20 years ago, in search of trading goods, he had been taken by his father on that long trip across the desert to the grasslands around Lake Chad, a dangerous journey but a successful one. They returned with goods that were traded for hard coin and many goats.

One does not wish to leave his family and this simple way of life, but a man must do what a man must do. It was time, now 20 years later, that he and his brother would again take that dangerous journey. Masoud would take his two eldest sons while his brother would take his eldest son.

The trip across the desert had proved successful. Now Masoud had twenty black children that could be traded for many goats, other goods, hard coin, and a nice piece of cloth for his wife. Masoud felt the pride of being a provident husband and father.

• • •

"Serena," Culligan said, "I saw a party in the distance. Curious, I sat and waited. When they were west of me and heading north, I saw there were five adults and they were herding four Burro's and a pack of children. They were slavers—I could have said it was none of my business—but still, I arose to my feet and moved in a parallel direction keeping pace with them. When they stopped, I stopped."

Masoud was well-armed for an Arab man, having both a fine muzzle-loading rifle and a cap-and-ball pistol. Masoud strode out to meet the danger. One must protect one's property. When they were within 200 yards of each other Culligan raised his Sharps. At that distance it was an easy shot. The shot took Masoud in the chest. As the blackness descended, Masoud's last thoughts were for his wife and children.

Masoud's brother, also having a long gun, came forward. Carefully, he crawled the last 50 yards to his brother. Seeing his brother was dead, he gathered up his weapons and, on hands and knees, began the trip back to their Party. Fifty yards out, and the stranger nowhere to be seen, he rose to his feet to sprint back. The bullet took him in the middle of his back.

• • •

The three young Arabs panicked; they were in siege. Keeping the donkeys and the children between them and Culligan's last known position, they hunkered down for the night.

"In daylight," Culligan said, "I had scoped out my next position and when a cloud passed in front of the moon I scurried to a new position a little more to the southeast of their position. Morning, the rising sun was at my back. I shot two of them.

"The blood lust was on me. When the children started to sing I looked up and sure enough, the last Arab was making a run for it. I shot him.

"At the time, I thought I was freeing naked children from a life of slavery. The truth is the killing that last Arab was unnecessary."

"So this is the crime, Serena said, "That troubles you?"

"Not so much."

Serena looked to Cheruni. "Tell me what happened out there."

"The others had been taken from a village in the grasslands. My parents and I lived alone in the desert. Massoud killed both my parents. The knots on the loops they put around my neck were too tight to unravel. Five days after I was taken, Culligan, my new father, killed every one of the slavers. He cut the first boy loose, handed him a knife, and watched as the boy freed us. I was the youngest and the last to be cut free."

"For myself," Culligan said, "I took a sack of millet and a waterbag."

Cheruni said, "The other children gathered up all the weapons, took all the slavers clothing, the donkeys, everything. When they went to leave, I tried to go with them. They pushed me down. When they left, I stayed sitting on the ground. I was lost. Then my new Father walked up, reached out his hand and I took it."

"So," Serena said, "that's how this came about."

"She was not of their tribe," Culligan said, "and was staggering with exhaustion. I took a drink from my canteen, then offered her a drink while I held onto the canteen. She took a drink. Then I turned Cheruni around, hoisted her up to set her on my backpack and she lost control and peed down the back of my neck."

Serena laughed while Cheruni ducked her head and put her hands over her eyes.

"That evening I boiled some of the grain and fed the two of us. I laid out my blanket, rolled onto it and I motioned for her to crawl on. She did. Bravest little girl I ever saw. I turned, put my back to her back."

"And?"

"And in time we reached a town sitting on the banks of the Nile called Bohen. Cheruni was still naked while all the town children there were wearing clothes. The men were looking me over and not too friendly.

"Cheruni had her left hand tucked into my belt in back. It was getting serious and then Cheruni began speaking. One of them, shorter than the others, understood her. Cheruni talked and he listened and nodded. Then he talked to the others in what I think was another language. Their faces softened. They were jabbering back and forth. Cheruni, at one point, held up five fingers. What was that about?"

"I was telling them that you killed five slavers."

"At another point you held up five fingers four times."

"That was telling them that there had been that many of us children."

"The one wearing the red fez on his head came up. He had not spoken. In English he said: 'She says that you killed five slavers and she thinks that you are now her father.'"

"I relaxed some, cupped the back of her head, and said, 'I do not speak her language. Tell her that she is now my daughter and I am her father.'

"The red fez told the others and the short man told Cheruni."

"When we reached the river," Cheruni said, "you bought me a yellow dress, a pair of sandals, and a turban. I love wearing pretty clothes. You took me to a café, everyone smiled, and we had food and drink. By boat we came from Bohen all the way down the Nile to Cairo and caught a boat to Marseilles, then, by carriage, we came to you, my new mother."

Culligan said, "I left nineteen children armed with two muzzle-loading rifles, and five cap'n ball revolvers. I remembered Abraham Leibowitz telling me that there were almost 200 different ethnic groups in the land, all jockeying for position and power. What had I done? Had my arming this group been a good thing, giving them the means to protect themselves, or was it a bad thing, allowing them to prey on others? I think it was a bad thing and that is what troubles me."

• • •

Twenty years ago, the stream running through their Scottish property had been a decent trout stream and had encouraged the spawning of salmon. The stream was now dead to fish. The years of the hooves of too many cattle, too many horses and too many sheep, having trampled down the containing banks, allowed the stream to spread so wide that the stream was no more than two inches deep in most locations.

At considerable expense, Culligan was restoring the stream as a habitant for fish. Culligan was sinking his roots down deep.

Serena said, "Cheruni has been telling me that she wants a little brother or sister. She is going to get her wish. Cully, I am with child."

• • •

Culligan was working with the crew planting deciduous saplings along the restored creek bank when Maisy's young son Rodney came running towards them shouting, "Mister Culligan! Mister Culligan, Sir!"

Culligan ran to meet him. The boy was breathless. Taking a breath, the boy said, "It's Cheruni Sir. She ran home from the school. I ran with her. She has blood on her legs and the back of her dress."

Culligan took off running. Maisy was holding Cheruni's hands while Serena applied salve to the bleeding welts on Seruni's buttocks. When Culligan arrived, looking at him, Serena said, "The schoolmaster did this. Then he ordered her to return to her seat. She ran home instead."

Cheruni said, "I never begged, I never cried, *he did not make me cry.*"

Culligan went for his gun.

Serena said, "Cully, for Christ's sake! This is SCOTLAND! You kill him and you will have to flee Scotland, and leaving the two of us behind, you will still be the Lone Wolf; is this what you want?"

. . . Cully slowly shook his head. "That's what I did when Cassy was so hurting. Not this time. Get the buggy ready." He left his gun.

• • •

The school children heard the clop, clop, clop, clop of a trotter pulling a buggy. It stopped in front of the school. Slow steps were heard on the porch. They stopped in front of the door . . . Then the door exploded off its hinges. "CHILDREN OUT!"

Children flew out the door but then watched from the doorway and windows. The schoolmaster grabbed up the stove poker but it did no good, Culligan caught it on its way down and threw it in the corner. He threw the schoolmaster across the room and against the wall. When the schoolmaster tried to run out the door, Culligan caught him and bounced him off the blackboard. Picking up one of the switches the schoolmaster had been drying out behind the stove, Culligan advanced on the schoolmaster who cowered and began to blubber.

"You beat my little child bloody and she did not cry. You cry even before you get hit. God! You are pathetic!"

Young Rodney and Cheruni had been the first children to reach the window. Rodney shouted, "Crybaby!" All seventeen children began to shout "Crybaby! Crybaby!"

"The only thing stopping me from beating you now is that I might not stop. The next time we meet I am going to give you a serious beating. God! You make my skin crawl!" Culligan threw the switch in the corner and walked out.

• • •

Cheruni, in the buggy, lying face-down on the comforter across the laps of Serena and Culligan, felt safe. Young Rodney as the footman, rode proud while standing upright in back and holding onto the roof of the carriage. "Rodney's parents," Culligan said, "may be servants, but he is a brave lad and he is clever. Wintertime, let's take him with us when we return to France. He stood up for Cheruni and I will see to it that he goes to college and he will graduate . . . I am going to see to that."

"The Lone Wolf," Serena said, "has now become a Country Gentleman— has taken a family— and is no longer the Lone Wolf."